W9-ATM-138

A. 5.

AMPFIRE
HOST
TORIES

ne Haunting Tales

Geordie Telfer

GHOST
HOUSE

House Books

© 2012 by Ghost House Books
First printed in 2012   10 9 8 7 6 5 4 3 2 1
Printed in Canada

All rights reserved. No part of this work covered by the copy
hereon may be reproduced or used in any form or by any me
graphic, electronic or mechanical—without the prior writte
of the publishers, except for reviewers, who may quote brie
Any request for photocopying, recording, taping or storage
tion retrieval systems of any part of this work shall be direc
to the publisher.

The Distributor: Lone Pine Publishing
2311 – 96 Street
Edmonton, AB T6N 1G3
Canada

Websites: www.ghostbooks.net
          www.lonepinepublishing.com

Library and Archives Canada Cataloguing in Publication

Telfer, Geordie
      Campfire ghost stories : the haunting tales / Geord

ISBN 978-1-55105-870-2

      1. Ghost stories, Canadian (English). I. Title.

PS8639.E427C34 2012   C813'.6   C20

Editorial Director: Nancy Foulds
Project Editor: Sheila Quinlan
Production Manager: Gene Longson
Layout and Production: Alesha Braitenbach
Cover Design: Gerry Dotto
Front Cover Images: fire and background © Ja
© Victor Soares | Dreamstime.com; flamir
iStockphoto; sky - © Photos.com
Back Cover Images: sky © Hemera Techn

We acknowledge the financial support c
through the Canada Book Fund (CBF)

Canadian   Patrimoine
Heritage   canadien

PC: 1

Contents

4: The SALIGIA Cycle

Foreword

Ghost stories can frighten us in two ways. First there is the ghost itself, the experience of being haunted. In these cases, it is the experience that is the scary thing—the eerie sensations that result as we imagine actually waking up to see a ghostly figure sitting silently in the corner. Second though, and sometimes equally frightening, are the implications for the human characters who are being haunted. In the pages that follow, you will meet living, breathing characters whose tragic flaws are often far more frightening than the ghosts who visit them.

The stories in this book are divided into three sections.

Campfire Ghosts: This section features tales that actually take place in or around camp settings. If you're going camping and want spooky tales that echo your actual surroundings, this is the section for you.

Ghosts in the Modern World: Here are hauntings in the world of today—online dating, uncooperative computer printers and graffiti-strewn alleyways form the backdrops for these tales, peopled with types we all know and haunted by ghosts whose motivations aren't always clear.

A Ghostly Miscellany: This is truly a mix-and-match grab bag of ghostly tales that concludes with a themed "cycle" of stories loosely inspired by the Seven Deadly Sins—read 'em and weep, as the card-sharps say.

Tips for Reading Ghost Stories Aloud

1) Practise. Whether you read a lot or a little, reading aloud to an audience is a whole different ball of wax than reading silently to yourself. Pick the story (or stories) you want to read ahead of time. Then practise reading them aloud to an empty room before you try it out in front of others.

2) Breathe. If you find that you're prone to nervousness, even when reading aloud to a few close friends, don't forget to breathe. Not only will this help to calm you down, but it will also give you greater control over your voice as you read the words. Or, let your jumpy nerves contribute to the atmosphere you create. After all, these are ghost stories with some scary bits.

3) Read ahead. The more you practise, the better you'll get. Eventually you'll be comfortable keeping your eyes a few words ahead of the words you're actually speaking aloud. It'll help you to see what's coming and prepare you for a shift in tone or delivery if a scary bit is coming.

4) Follow punctuation and italics. If you find your tongue tripping over itself when reading aloud, commas, periods and dashes will often sort things out for you. Keep an eye out for these and other indicators. Think of them as road signs that tell you how fast and in what direction to go. In some stories there are *italics* at the scary bits (or the bits that are supposed to be scary). You don't have to go crazy with

your voice when you get to these parts, but you may want to add some sort of emphasis or make a subtle change in tone.

5) Take your time. Remember that even more than scaring people, you're setting out to entertain them, to go on a journey together. Whether there's a moment of slam-bang scariness, eerie uncertainty or simple resolution, most people like to be read aloud to, no matter what the outcome of the story is. The actual process of reading aloud to other people is where the value of the experience lies, more so than frightening them into their sleeping bags.

6) Have a beverage nearby. Nothing is worse than reading aloud while you're thirsty or have a frog in your throat. Coffee, tea and other hot liquids are not recommended.

7) Let the words do the work. It's not like you have to memorize these stories; the words are all right there in front of you. If your audience doesn't like the story, just blame me.

8) Figure out what your reading light is going to be. It's all very well to practise in a well-lit room, but you may discover that, in the darkness of the woods, the words are almost impossible to see. You may be thinking to yourself that the light of the campfire will provide all the illumination you need, but you'll probably want to face your audience, which means facing the fire—the pages of the book are going to be in the dark. You could tilt the book downward, but bowing your head like that and reading aloud will strain your voice. I recommend simply sitting sideways or getting either one of those little clip-lights that attach to the book or a miner-style light that you can wear on your head. A flashlight, you ask? Hmm…maybe, but turning the pages of the book with

a flashlight in your hand is kind of awkward and tends to break the flow of the story if the light is dipping up and down every time you turn the page. But it does give you the option of pointing your flashlight scarily up at your own face at the conclusion of the story.

9) Finally, have fun. All of the above tips are there to be tried and then forgotten as you develop your own style of reading aloud and discover what a refreshing escape it can be, both for you and your audience. Happy (or scary) reading!

1
Campfire Ghosts

Ghost of the Haunted Wood

Ever since they met on a springtime camping trip, Catherine and James had been wishfully eyeing each other. But as spring blossomed into summer and the summer leaves fell into autumn, neither one had mustered up the courage to make a move. It was driving their friends crazy—why couldn't one just slip into the other's sleeping bag some night and be done with it?

The friends who had introduced them were vibrant out-doorsy types who did everything as a group. This hearty band of adventurers climbed mountains *en masse*, canoed like a flotilla of voyageurs and circled campfires like one big happy tribe. Collectively they decided that the only solution to the "CJ sitch" (short for "Catherine and James situation") was to go on a winter camp in the Haunted Wood.

The Haunted Wood was a campsite reputedly haunted by some sort of deranged spirit—a murderous psychopath, a treasure-seeking lake pirate, a whimpering child—something along those lines. No one in the group was quite clear on who or what the spirit was supposed to be, nor did they particularly care, since none of them believed it for a second. What they did believe was that a cold winter night, an alleged ghost and a shared tent were ingredients that could not fail but to mix happily into something that might be a meaningful relationship for Catherine and James.

For their part, Catherine and James were of one mind, though they'd never discussed it—each really liked the other and didn't want to rush what might be a good thing. While the surrounding circle of friends were all extroverts, Catherine and James were introverts, and they knew it. Besides, when they looked into one another's eyes, each could see the other's feelings. They were confident and didn't feel the need to hurry.

So, the winter camp in the Haunted Wood was set for the first weekend in December. With typical efficiency, the collective had sent around little diagrams showing who would be sleeping in which tents. Catherine and James rolled their eyes when they found out they'd been assigned to share a tent, but only because it seemed like such an obvious ploy—not because they minded.

The group got to the campsite around two in the afternoon, and the next few hours were a busy bustle to pitch the tents, build a fire and get supper ready. By the time dusk fell, their bellies were full and the tribe had settled into the familiar circle around the campfire. By turns everyone donned the raggedy toque they had dubbed the storyteller's hat and made up tales intended to frighten Catherine and James into one another's arms: the Ghost of the Haunted Wood was a skeletal wraith that preyed on lonely souls; the Ghost of the Haunted Wood was a spectral shadow that never picked on lovers; the Ghost of the Haunted Wood was a wavering glow that foreshadowed...joyous events? Everyone agreed that the last one was pretty lame, but now the storyteller's hat had come to James. After James it would go to Catherine. The two of them had, in advance, worked out a plan for this moment.

"Well," said James, "I'm going for a walk." And then, standing and turning to Catherine he said, "Would you like to come?"

In the stunned silence, Catherine leapt to her feet and the two of them scurried away from the fire's glow. By the time the hoots, cat-calls and wolf-whistles began, they were already beyond the clearing and into the woods.

For the first few minutes they didn't say anything, but just walked along listening to their footsteps crunching in the snow. The moon shone through the skeletal tree branches to cast an eerie crisscross of shadows all around them. A sudden gust of wind moved the branches, and the surrounding shadows shifted like ghostly wraiths. In a heartbeat their gloved hands found one another in the darkness.

"Do you believe these woods are haunted?" James asked Catherine, squeezing her hand.

"You mean do I think all these shadows are skeletal wraiths who prey on lonely souls?" replied Catherine, squeezing back. "No more than you do."

A sudden shadow seemed pass over them and was gone again. They turned to face one another. Catherine asked, "Do you believe that was a ghostly shadow that won't pick on lovers?"

"I think it was an owl," said James. "And what's more, I really like you."

"I know," said Catherine. "Me too."

James was surprised by how warm her lips were and how sweet they tasted. This went on for quite a while until they both realized they were forgetting to breathe and pulled apart for a few seconds. They stood there, listening to the pounding of their hearts and watching the moon shimmer on the snow.

"Do you suppose the moonlight on the snow is a ghostly glow that foreshadows a joyous event?" asked James.

Catherine looked at him, her eyes shining, and said, "I think it very well might be."

Then they each pulled off one glove so that they could hold hands properly. They walked along like that for a bit. Presently, they stopped and Catherine looked at him with the playful expression that, over the months, he'd learned to love. "Come and find me!" And with that, she dashed off through the snow and into the trees.

James chased after her and quickly discovered that she was better at hiding than he was at seeking. Several minutes passed as he snuck up on trees and delved into shadows without finding her, and then, with a shudder of dread, he realized that he was lost.

Now all of the shadows seemed like they *were* ghosts, and the silence of the winter forest at night, which had seemed so serene, felt like a suffocating vapour. With his heartbeat thundering in his ears he stumbled through the moonlight, panic rising in his chest. Every branch that scratched his face was a skeletal hand and every shadow a phantom tormentor. Were all of those stories actually true? He was so panicked he never even thought to call out for help. He lost track of time. Had he been lost for minutes or hours? He checked his watch; they had walked away from the campfire at about 8:00 PM; it was now 9:30. Well that wasn't too long, but still, he was completely lost. How was he going to find Catherine? How would they find their way back to camp?

And then he saw her, standing in a clearing.

"I'm right here," she said. "Let's go back."

"I got lost," he said.

"I'll show you the way." She put her hand in his. It was freezing.

"Your hand is like ice."

"I lost my glove after I took it off."

"Here, have mine." He slipped his glove onto her hand. "And you're limping," he said.

"I twisted my ankle. No big deal."

Leaning on each other they made their way back, their feet crunching reassuringly in the snow. Back at camp the fire was out and the rest of the tents were dark, their occupants long abed. Catherine and James stopped in front of their shared tent and hugged each other tight.

Finally James pulled back to look at Catherine. "I never want to be apart from you," he said.

"We'll always be together," she said, and with that they went into the tent.

The next morning, James awoke alone. He noticed his lone glove next to his sleeping bag. Where was Catherine? And for that matter, how had they both managed to fit into his single-person sleeping bag? It was barely big enough for one, let alone two campers. He pulled on his boots and quietly emerged from the tent. Dawn was just starting to creep over the tree tops. The rest of the camp was still asleep. He breathed in the quiet and was contemplating the day ahead when his heart skipped a beat—*there was only one set of footprints leading through the snow and into their tent.*

They found her at the bottom of a jagged cliff, one ankle horribly twisted. In her playful flight from James, she must have run right over the edge and plunged straight down onto the snow-covered rocks. The glass of her wristwatch had been smashed by the fall but the hour and minute hands were intact—they had stopped at 9:00. James' other glove lay in the snow beside her. She was as calm and beautiful in death as she had been in life. James was surprised at how cold her lips were.

The Haunted Boyfriend

Gwen felt lucky to have met David. He seemed almost too good to be true—good looking, gainfully employed and kind, so kind. They had met in the baggage retrieval area at the airport—not exactly a setting that promises romance, but when he had seen her struggling with her heavy luggage and offered to lend a hand, she had been only too happy to accept. And so with this act of kindness, their romance was set in motion.

From what she'd seen in the months since, his kindness was sincere. When they met at the airport he had been coming back from charity work in Africa, where he was digging wells for orphans (or something). Whenever they passed street beggars with outstretched hands, David dug in his pocket for change, or if it was cold he would try to direct them to the nearest homeless shelter. If they were on the bus he was the first to give up his seat for elderly patrons. If they were driving he would never hesitate to let other drivers go first. And when she took him to meet her parents one weekend, he helped to tidy up and do the dishes.

If there was one downside to dating David, it was that his charity work meant he travelled a lot. When he was gone Gwen missed him and tried to make time for just the two of them whenever she could. That summer had been a particularly busy one with David continent-hopping almost non-stop, building a school here, purifying drinking water there and otherwise helping the hungry, the downtrodden and the generally less fortunate.

So when Labour Day came and went with David away yet again, Gwen didn't ask him if they could go camping the next weekend, she *told* him. It was odd, she thought to herself as she packed, he knew she loved camping, but whenever she had tried to get him to go before, he had always found some reason not to go—either some last-minute charity event or exhaustion from travel or some other excuse that seemed beyond reproach. This time Gwen was having none of it; the season was over and they would have the campground all to themselves.

Once the tent was up and they'd eaten supper, Gwen grabbed David's hand and pulled him off for a walk through the forest. She breathed deeply, savouring the scents of the woods and soaking up the quiet.

"Isn't it nice to have some time to ourselves? Just us and no one else," she smiled up at him.

"It sure is," David agreed kindly, though somewhat unconvincingly.

"Are you okay?" Gwen asked.

"Yes. It's…er…it's just been so busy lately that I'm…er…kind of gobsmacked by finally being here with you—just the two of us."

Gwen couldn't tell for sure, but he seemed to put sort of an odd emphasis on the words "just the two of us."

It was dark when they got back to camp. As soon as she saw the tent, Gwen gasped. *It was lit from inside.* She knew she hadn't turned on her flashlight before they left.

"David," she whispered. "Look."

David looked. He didn't seem upset or startled, but he certainly looked a bit grim. "I'll check it out," he said.

"Be careful!" hissed Gwen, her eyes wide with concern.

It happened right before her eyes—David went up to the tent, and at the very instant he unzipped the flaps, the light went out.

"There's nothing here," he said (a bit wearily, Gwen thought, almost as though he had known there wouldn't be anything there).

In the tent, Gwen looked around for the flashlight or anything else that could have lit up the tent. She found no explanation and discovered that the flashlight was still packed at the bottom of the her backpack. She thought it was very strange and said so to David.

"Er…fireflies maybe," he said, kindly but lamely.

They settled down to sleep and Gwen drifted off listening to the pleasant sounds of the nearby lake and the wind in the tree tops…and woke up suddenly in the pitch dark to *the sound of the tent's zipper being slowly drawn open*, tooth by agonizing tooth. Maybe David was going to pee, but no, he was right there snoring softly beside her. She grabbed the flashlight, turned it on and shouted, "Who's there?!"

David awoke with a start beside her. "What is it?" he said groggily.

"Someone's out there and they're trying to come in the tent," she said, and then, more loudly for the benefit of whoever was outside, "We're all hunters, you know! All six of us have twelve-gauge shotguns and we sleep with them loaded."

"I'm sure there's nobody there," said David.

"Well look, the zipper is half down." There in the beam of her flashlight were the half-undone tent flaps.

"Well…uh…" said David, "I think I remember forgetting to close the zipper all the way when we went to bed."

"*I* closed it when we went to bed, and *I* closed it all the way," said Gwen.

David took the flashlight and poked it out the tent flaps, looking around. "Well there's nobody there now." And with that, he firmly zipped up the flaps and got back into his sleeping bag.

Gwen soon fell into a restless sleep through which she kept an iron grip on the flashlight. Again she woke with a start in the darkness. This time she could hear something or someone outside, scraping against the material of the tent. She shook David awake.

"Listen," she said.

"It's just some tree branches," said David.

"We're camped in a clearing," she said.

Gwen clicked on the flashlight and screamed. Clearly visible were the bulges of five little fingers pressing on the tent canvas from outside and slowly clawing downward. Another set appeared on the other side of the tent. When the first shape of a distorted child's face pressed itself in at her through the material, she fainted. She didn't see the rest of them appear, nor was she conscious to hear David say, "Oh give it a rest already."

Gwen awoke to the acrid whiff of David's smelling salts (he kept some on him at all times in case of fainting seniors). The flashlight was on, and looking around she couldn't see anything out of the ordinary.

"What is going on here?" she demanded.

"Well, it's like this," said David with an air of resignation. "Everything that's been happening tonight is because of… well…it's my orphans."

"What?"

"Or more accurately, it's the ghosts of some orphans who follow me around."

"Ghosts?"

"Yup."

"Ghosts of orphans?"

"Yes."

"Where do they come from?"

"Oh, all over the place really. All the countries I go to."

"And why do they follow you?"

"Honestly? Because I let them."

Gwen looked incredulous. "Why?" she asked.

"Well, they had hard lives, and it doesn't seem right to deny them the pleasures of a mischievous afterlife. They've already had a really rough time of it, I'm not going to call in an exorcist. That would be unkind."

"How have your other girlfriends taken this news?"

"Not that well, really," said David with a sigh. "But the orphans seem to really like you."

"They do?"

"Oh sure, because you scare so easily."

Gwen didn't know how to respond to that. "And they only like to come out on camping trips, do they?"

"That's how they like to reveal themselves to new people, but now that you've seen them they'll probably come out a bit more when we're alone together."

"Honestly, I don't know if I want to be together," said Gwen.

"That's too bad," said David. "I do really like you."

"I really like you too, but I can't cope with a legion of little poltergeists."

"They prefer to be called disembodied spirits."

"Don't their ghostly hijinks disturb you?"

"It's not like they're at it all the time. Mainly whenever I start seeing someone, actually."

"Well I think that problem is about to end. I don't know if I can keep seeing you if this is what it's going to be like all the time."

"Er...well, here's the thing," said David with a tone of genuine remorse. "They find scaring you to be so much fun that they've decided to stop haunting me and start haunting you."

And even as he spoke, she heard a little raspy voice at her ear whisper, "*Gwen.*"

The Eye of the Beholder

The trio of hikers forced themselves up the steep mountain path, sweating, slipping and swearing. They'd been at it for hours, and their backs and ankles ached from the sharp incline. It was foggy, too, making their clothes cling to their bodies and the moisture from the surrounding air condense like sweat on their faces and foreheads.

At last the steep angle began to lessen and they emerged onto an alpine meadow, waist-deep in long summer grasses. Here, they stopped and filled their canteens from a trickling stream that wended its way cheerily through the long grass. They stood together silently, sipping from their canteens and catching their breath.

They were all pretty close in age—latish twenties: Callie, sturdy and blonde, a veteran hiker and all-round outdoors-woman; Mark, her boyfriend, an aspiring painter who, luckily for their relationship, enjoyed painting rugged landscapes; and Alex, Mark's older brother, a self-styled local historian of the nearby mountains and the valley communities they sheltered. This was the seventh time they had climbed Widow's Peak in two years. Callie would have done it anyway, Mark did it to be with Callie, and Alex…well, Alex was on a quest.

Alex was determined to discover the fate of Arthur Hendrick, an eccentric painter who vanished in 1922. Like Mark, Hendrick had loved to paint the outdoors. His vivid colours and vibrant compositions, so reflective of the local wilderness, had garnered him a national reputation. But then Hendrick had seemed to come a bit unhinged. He started spending most of his time in a tiny hut somewhere on or around Widow's Peak and refused to tell anyone where it was. On the rare occasions that he wandered down into town to pick up his mail-order paints from the post office and buy some food, he had a haunted, unbalanced look about him. He told baffled listeners that "it" was after him and went on to spin tall tales of a gigantic spirit that loomed out of the fog at him, floating just out of his reach, sometimes 50 or 100 feet tall! It tormented him, seeming to copy his every move, never harming him or making any sounds, but always there, looming, towering over and frightening him with its immense size, like a ghostly giant climbed down from its beanstalk.

The townies just assumed Hendrick was drunk, for every trip to town for pigments and foodstuffs was bolstered by a generous purchase of whisky. But their opinion of him changed just before he disappeared. Hendrick was only in his late thirties and had a shaggy head of rich brown hair that any local could spot a block away. But one day when he stumbled down off the mountain path, the people were shocked to see that, in under a month, Hendrick's hair had turned as white as snow. Whatever it was that scared Arthur Hendrick, he, at least, was convinced that it was real.

And Alex, diligent researcher and historical detective that he was, had actually managed to find photos in the local paper that seemed to prove this sudden change of hair colour. Now, based on their previous six trips up Widow's Peak and all of his research, Alex was convinced they were getting close to finding Hendrick's hut. For Alex, it was a case of simple historical discovery—could they find Arthur Hendrick's hut and maybe even his body? For Mark, it was a case of wanting to discover the fate of a fellow painter. Also, Hendrick had infamously disappeared leaving behind neither immediate family nor a will—if there happened to be a few canvases lying around that had somehow survived nearly 100 years in the elements, well, they would be worth a lot of money. And as for Callie, it was one of her favourite trails to hike, and whenever anyone mentioned the massive ghosts that Hendrick had said were haunting him, she seemed to get a knowing look in her eye, though neither Mark nor Alex had ever been able to get her to say what was on her mind.

"Well," said Callie, capping her water bottle, "if we're going to make it to the top before dark, we should push on." They all took one last look at the pleasant, fog shrouded meadow and made ready to continue. Each of the other times they had climbed the trail they had stopped here too—it made a perfect resting place because it was almost exactly halfway to the top. The meadow was flat and open but surrounded by dense forest on all sides, with the entrances to the trail going up and down just visible as dim openings in the trees.

They had just reached the entrance to the path to resume the hike up when Mark stopped suddenly. "You know," he said, "if I were a crazy recluse painter and wanted access to all the different mountain peaks and sights, I'd set up camp right around here. Think about it: your hut or lean-to or whatever would be relatively sheltered, as opposed to being blasted by wind and rain if you were out on the side of the mountain. You could hike up to the top of the mountain or down to town equally easily, and you'd have easy access to the stream."

Alex nodded. They had been operating on the assumption that Hendrick would have needed access to the little stream for his water, so they'd looked all over the mountain, wherever it trickled down, but they'd never actually thought to stop and search the area around the meadow. "You're right," said Alex. "Let's split up and look around the edge of the meadow."

So, the afternoon wore on. Hours went by as they poked into thickets of underbrush and hunted through the trees for any sign of Arthur Hendrick. Just as the sun was beginning to sink and the fog was getting thicker, Alex and Callie, from their separate search areas, heard Mark's exuberant "Whoo-hoooo!" They saw him emerge from the trees on the far side of the clearing and rushed over to where he stood. Mark led them back through the trees to a spot where, without warning, the ground fell away, and there, perched on the side of the mountain but still sheltered by the dense woods, were the remains of a wooden hut. Amazingly, though the roof had caved in in one spot, the walls were still standing and the three of them stuck their heads through the open doorway at the same time—and gasped.

There, seated in a rough chair made from logs and behind an oversized easel also made of logs, sat a skeleton. The animals and the elements had long since stripped it clean of flesh, but on the floor, close to its feet, was a paintbrush. There was even a blackened canvas on the easel, seemingly nailed there by its painter either out of madness or determination. They stepped into the hut to get a better look and all three of them whipped out their cameras and started taking pictures.

They gasped a second time when they looked through the gap in the wall that had evidently served as Hendrick's window. In fair weather it would have been a spectacular view of the side of the mountain, but shrouded in fog as it was today, it made one feel as if one was floating in eternity.

"This must have been where he saw the giant ghosts," said Alex.

"Look at this!" said Mark. With careless disregard for archaeological niceties, he had started moving the fallen sections of rotten roof wood and had uncovered something that appeared to be a large greasy boulder tucked away in one corner of the hut.

"What is it?" asked Callie.

"It's something wrapped up in oilskin," said Mark. He pulled out his pocketknife and commenced poking here and cutting there until, layer by layer, he stripped the protective, oiled cloth away to find a dozen neatly stacked canvases. He delicately pulled one out and they gasped again. The colours were full and bright, Hendrick's brush strokes still clear in the thick pigment. It unmistakably showed the view out the window—there were patches of blue sky with some nearby mountain peaks just visible peaking up through a thick sea of fog. In the centre was an unmistakably human figure, a shadow radiating a huge halo and, to judge from the perspective, absolutely massive in size. None of them said anything. They took a look at the other canvases, all of which showed similar, frightening renderings.

"Check it out," said Alex. He stuck his hand between two of the paintings and pulled out a little diary. It was filled with dense, tiny, utterly mad handwriting. Alex flipped to the last entry.

May 8th, 1922

It comes out of the fog and lurks, mirroring my every move. It vanishes when I retreat into the hut, but when I venture out it is there again, mute, massive and towering. What does it want from me? I am becoming too frightened to go outside, so now I sit here with my easel, peering out the window. Even when I am inside

I can still see it floating in front of me in my mind's eye. The image is burned into my mind. I fear that wherever I go, whatever I see and whatever I try to paint, this spectre will haunt my brush if not my eyes.

I am too frightened to go outside now and so I think I shall die here, in this chair, behind this easel, painting the thing that is not there, trying, trying and failing to capture its spectral essence with mere paint and canvas. I think

The diary ended there. Seemingly in mid thought, Hendrick had chosen to consign the diary to a package of canvases for the next 90 years.

"Hey guys, look at this!" It was Callie calling from outside. While Alex and Mark had been engrossed in the diary she had slipped out of the hut. They went to find her and both of their hearts skipped a beat—*there were three gigantic spectral figures emerging from the fog.* They must have been 100 feet tall. They seemed to shine with a ghostly aura. Rays of light rippled from their sides. What mysterious world did they come from? What did they see? Why were they here? What did they want? The three ghosts floated there in front of their earthly counterparts.

"Oh geez, the middle one's waving at us," said Mark.

"No!" said Callie. "It's me." From their positions on either side of her, Mark and Alex looked over to see that Callie was indeed waving, and so was the middle ghost of the three gigantic spectres. "They're Brocken spectres!" she said.

"They're what inspectors?" asked Alex.

"They're optical illusions from the angle of the sun hitting the fog—they're our shadows, but they're all distorted and they look like they're giants."

"Hey, mine's waving too," said Mark, crazily waving his arm back and forth. "And shimmering too!"

Alex turned to Callie. "You knew the whole time that Hendrick was seeing a Brocken spectre, didn't you?"

"I had my suspicions," said Callie. "I'd seen them once before when I was hiking up here in college. You just need the right conditions, and with all the fogs that roll in up here, it seemed like a definite possibility."

"Well," said Mark, "we have some very valuable paintings to carry down the side of the hill, and then we'll have to figure out a fitting memorial to Arthur Hendrick."

They turned toward the hut once more and the massive spectres faded away.

Try Not to Scratch

As they scrambled through the thick underbrush of the forest, Drea and Allan struggled to remember a time when they *hadn't* been running. As they slapped and swatted at the thick cloud of mosquitoes tormenting them, they tried to remember a time when there *hadn't* been a little cyclone of whining, irritating insects swirling around them, buzzing in their ears and darting at their eyes. As they scratched at a thousand different itching bites, they wondered what it was like *not* to feel twisting, jaw-gritting rage at countless tiny, uncomprehending tormentors.

"I think there's a pond in a clearing up here," said Allan. "If we can get to it, maybe we can jump in and get away from them."

"Didn't you say that, like, an hour ago?" gasped Drea.

"Maybe. I can't even think straight anymore. How long have we been out here, anyway?"

"I don't know. Feels like days, but it's probably only been a couple of hours."

It had started out as a nice walk in the woods, punctuated by a pleasantly pointless metaphysical discussion about whether animals have souls.

"If animals do have souls," Drea joked lightly, "then I'm in trouble, because I don't even know how many insects I've killed in my lifetime."

"Me too," said Allan.

Then, as if on cue, Drea and Allan were beset from all sides by a ravening swarm of hungry mosquitoes. Their shorts and t-shirts left plenty of exposed skin for the little blood-suckers to drink from. In a few seconds both them were covered in itchy bites, and a minute or two after that, both of them were covered in bright red blood splats, each one representing the life of a mosquito terminated by their swatting hands. They started to run.

Now, what seemed like hours later, it no longer seemed to make a difference that they tried to squash the bugs. It was as if, aside from the itching and buzzing, the mosquitoes weren't actually there.

"I can see the clearing up ahead," rasped Allan. "Come on."

At long last they emerged into the clearing and stopped dead in their tracks. There was indeed a pond. Calm, clear and placid, it looked like the ideal place to seek cooling, soothing refuge from a swarm of seemingly vengeful mosquitoes—or it would have were it not for the two bodies floating face down in it. They drifted imperceptibly in the still water, almost calmly, peacefully.

Drea gasped. "Allan," she whimpered, "*they're wearing our clothes.*"

Allan looked down at their attire and then back at the bodies in the pond. It was true. He was wearing faded blue cut-offs and a tie-dye t-shirt—so was one body floating in the pond. Drea was wearing brown shorts with cargo pockets and a white t-shirt with a windbreaker tied around her waist—so was the other body floating in the pond. Cringing and nervous, they waded into the water and flipped the bodies over—sure enough, their own faces, bloated and bitten, looked back at them.

"We're dead!" said Drea, sounding more surprised than terrified.

"So we're ghosts," said Allan.

"We must have run in here to get away from the mosquitoes and drowned," said Drea.

"I wonder how long we've been doing this," said Allan.

"So, if we're ghosts," said Drea, thinking it through, "that means those mosquitoes are ghosts too." As she said this, the spectral swarm of insects emerged from the woods and hovered at the edge of the pond.

"I guess animals do have souls," said Allan. "These must be all the mosquitoes we killed in our lifetime."

"And here they come," said Drea.

The swarm was on the move again and so were Allan and Drea. Ghosts or not, the itching was real and so was the whining, irritating drone of the insects. Now, as they moved away from the pond, fleeing into the woods, the memory of what they had just found began to fade and their plight was once more a breathless, itchy, panicked dash to escape—at any cost.

As they scrambled through the thick underbrush of the forest, Drea and Allan struggled to remember a time when they *hadn't* been running...

Summer Haunt

Every summer for as long as they could remember, the Hanté family had found their way back to their favourite campground at Spectral Lake. It was a popular little cluster of gravel lots for camper vans. Each of the 10 lots faced out directly onto the lake, and toward the rear of each one there was a fire pit and an electrical outlet on a post. It was very civilized.

The Hanté family numbered four. Betty and Don were mother and father. Bobby and Sally were brother and sister, nine and six years old respectively. Each summer everyone looked forward to meeting another family with kids so that Bobby and Sally would have some summer playmates. They were an outgoing pair and loved to show the new friends they made all the secrets of the lake—the best places to hide, the best spots to swim and the best trees to climb. Betty and Don loved to watch their children meet and make friends with other kids. It kind of made up for the fact that any adults they'd ever met at Spectral Lake completely ignored the whole Hanté family—Betty and Don assumed they were a bunch of snobs.

So Betty and Don were happy when they saw Bobby and Sally coming back to the campsite with a boy about Bobby's age. Their parents had seen the little trio emerge from between two camper vans a couple of lots over and smiled at each other as they watched their offspring excitedly pointing out the local features. When they arrived, Bobby did the introductions.

"Mom, Dad, this is Glen."

"Hello, Glen," said Betty and Don.

"Hi," said Glen, smiling broadly at them.

"Can Glen stay for supper?" Sally asked.

"If it's okay with his parents," said Betty.

"I asked. They said it was fine," said Glen.

"Then I'll fire up the barbecue," said Don, and matched the action to the words.

As Don cooked supper, Betty looked at her kids' new friend; he was a nice-looking boy with a light tan, cheery brown eyes and a mop of sun-stained blond hair, and he smiled easily and often. For all that, there was something a bit odd about him—he looked around the inside of their camper-van as though he'd never seen anything like it before.

"How do you like the old 'Hanté Camp-on-Wheels,' as we like to call it?" asked Don heartily.

"Er...it's cool," said Glen.

"Top of the line," said Don. "Windigo brand. The seats are Corinthian leather."

It was when they were eating that everyone began to truly suspect that Glen was something out of the ordinary. First he asked for a second hot dog, which no one thought was unusual, and they were happy to oblige. When he proceeded to ask for a hamburger after that, they assumed he was just a big eater. But after he had veritably inhaled a second burger and asked for a third with no appearance of slowing down, Betty and Don were starting to wonder if perhaps he was some sort of feral child raised by wolves, though his well-groomed appearance, good manners and obvious acquisition of language seemed to belie this hypothesis. Even after five helpings of sliced potatoes cooked in foil on the barbecue, Glen sounded all too eager when he asked if there was dessert. After a few s'mores, he thanked them politely, said he was still hungry and that he was going back to his parents' trailer for supper.

The Hantés looked at each other after he left.

"Well," said Betty, "Glen certainly can eat a lot, but he seems like a very nice boy."

"Maybe he's got a tapeworm," said Don.

"What's a tapeworm?" asked Bobby and Sally in one voice, and so the evening turned toward other topics until it was time for bed.

They awoke to Sally's screams at about three in the morning. Don fumbled around and flicked on the lights. Sally's eyes were as big as saucers and she was cowering in one corner of her bunk, trembling. Bobby was sitting on the edge of his mattress, his eyes wild, breathing heavy.

"It was Glen," he said. "He was asleep right there on the floor."

"And then he just disappeared," said Sally.

"You were just dreaming," said Betty soothingly.

"Both of us?" said Bobby.

Neither Betty nor Don had any good explanation for this. They calmed both kids down as best they could, and everyone went back to sleep.

The next morning, the Hantés were eating breakfast around their folding table outside when Glen walked by. They all greeted him, and Betty and Don hoped he wouldn't invite himself to breakfast because they had only brought enough food for a week. Before they could say anything else, Glen came out with it.

"I had a weird dream last night," he said. "I dreamt I was lying on the floor of your camper-van. Then in the dream, Sally started screaming and I woke up."

The Hantés looked at each other, none of them really sure of what to say. Then they heard a woman's voice calling, "Glen, breakfast is ready!" and off he ran, much to the relief of Betty and Don, who were uneasily eyeing the pancakes.

Later that day, Bobby and Sally decided to go for a swim. Right in front of their trailer, in full view of their parents, they waded out into the lake. Sally stopped when the water was at her waist, maybe 18 inches deep. Bobby waded out a little further and stopped when the water was at his waist, perhaps two and a half or three feet deep. Pointing at a spot on the bottom roughly between them, Bobby said, "Look at that cool piece of quartz. Bet I can get it before you can."

And with that, both kids ducked their heads under the water—and came up screaming and sputtering with an inert third form between them: Glen. Betty and Don both ran into the water and helped drag the insensate Glen to dry land.

Sally, stumbling over her words, said, "We ducked under the water to get the stone and he was just *there*."

Bobby's voice trembled, "We could see everything. When we were looking at that stone he wasn't there, and then we went under the water and he *was*!"

Glen sputtered and spit out some water and opened his eyes. He looked around at all of them, and then they heard a woman's voice scream, "Glen!" In a second, both of Glen's parents were there.

"Are you okay?" asked his dad.

"Uh, I think so," said Glen, looking around as though searching for something.

The Hantés tried to introduce themselves, but Glen's father only had eyes for his son and Glen's mother appeared to be on the verge of an actual conniption, wailing tearfully and clutching her son to her breast, rocking back and forth like a mad woman.

"But Mom," they heard Glen say, "I'm fine."

"I know, I know, dear," his mother sobbed.

At lunch time the Hantés were sitting around the table outside again when Glen and his parents walked by, all of them peering rather blankly at the surrounding camper-vans.

"Hi, Glen," said Sally, a little fearfully but amicably enough. Glen and his parents had a strange blank look in their eyes as they looked right at the Hantés without seeming to see them.

Glen's father said to his mother, "They haven't made Windigos since the seventies." And then the three of them moved on in their odd, absent way.

"That does it," said Bobby. "I think they're ghosts."

"So do I," said Sally.

"And what's more," said Bobby, "I bet that Glen kid drowned here and his parents somehow died trying to save him and now all three of them haunt the lake."

"There's no such thing as ghosts," said Don.

"And that would explain why he could eat so much!" exclaimed Betty. "How can you fill up a ghost?"

"You're actually buying this?" said Don, looking at Betty.

"Either way," said Betty, "do you really want to spend any more time here?"

"We spend all of our summers here," protested Don.

"Let's at least go down to the registration office and see if anyone else has noticed anything weird," said Betty sensibly.

"It's five miles along the roadway to the registration office," said Don. Betty just looked at him. "Fine," he said. "We'll take the camper."

So they unplugged the electricity and tidied up their stuff and set off in the camper-van down the narrow winding road that led out to the highway where the campsite's registration office was. All of a sudden the camper-van began veering wildly.

"What the hell!" said Don as he fought to regain control of the vehicle.

"What's happening?!" shouted Betty.

"I don't know!" said Don.

"Look out!" cried Bobby and Sally together.

There, around a curve in front of them, had appeared the backs of Glen and his parents walking on the road toward the highway. The erratic movements of the camper-van were making it impossible for Don to control. He honked the horn to alert Glen's family, but they showed no signs of hearing.

"No!" they all cried in horror as the camper-van bore down on the walking family. They all braced themselves for the impact, but none came—*the forms of Glen and his parents briefly flashed through the interior of the camper-van as though they had passed right through it.*

Bobby and Sally turned to look out the rear window. "I told you they were ghosts!" shouted Bobby. "They're fine. They're still walking."

No one could quite remember what happened next, but they found themselves still inside the camper-van safely in the parking lot beside the registration office.

"What happened?" said Betty.

"I think Glen and his parents somehow saved us from dying," said Bobby.

Don sighed, opened the door and got out. The rest of them did likewise. Inside the registration office, they found

Glen and his parents talking to Mike, the kindly park ranger who had worked at the park as long as the Hantés been coming to it.

"Yes," said Mike to Glen's family. "It was a great tragedy. I knew them pretty well."

"What's Mike talking about?" asked Sally.

"Uh...Mom? Dad?" said Bobby. They turned to where Bobby was looking at a newspaper clipping pinned to a bulletin board.

Local services mark 30th anniversary of tragedy

Thirty years ago the Hanté family came to spend their summer vacation at Spectral Lake. Don and Betty Hanté started camping here in the early 1960s when they were dating. With the arrival of their two children, Bobby and Sally, the couple's annual trip became a family tradition—a welcome summer break from city life. In 1975, the Hantés bought a brand-new Windigo camper-van and pulled into one of the new lots by the lake.

But tragedy soon followed. Witnesses say that nine-year-old Bobby and six-year-old Sally were diving for stones when they both drowned. In a frantic attempt to get their children to a hospital in the hopes of resuscitating them, Don and Betty loaded the children into the Windigo and started out for town. But on the way, Don lost control of the vehicle when its stabilization bar broke, and the Windigo went off a cliff. Weak stabilizer (or "sway") bars were a major defect of the Windigo line and led to its discontinuation later that year.

Starting in 1976, campers began reporting ghostly encounters with the Hantés, who still apparently enjoy their summer vacations here. Some report seeing a spectral Windigo that can pass through solid objects and even people, leaving them unharmed. Others guests have reported odd dreams in which they seem to wake up in a strange, outdated camper-van to the screams of a frightened girl. Still others, who deny any foreknowledge of the legend, swear they have visited a friendly family of fellow campers who feed them vast quantities of curiously insubstantial food. And finally, on at least three occasions, the ghostly family has reportedly saved campers from drowning.

A candlelight vigil is scheduled at the Spectral Lake Campsites this Saturday evening at dusk. For more information call...

Bobby and Sally started crying. Don and Betty too.

You Think, Therefore It Is...

Harold Cuvier looked into the bathroom mirror. He bared his teeth and bloodied gums. He extended his index finger to wobble one of his loose incisors and then, knowing with dreadful certainty what would happen, grasped the tooth and yanked it out. He held it in front of him and regarded the string of red saliva that trailed like a gory vine from his upper gum to the tooth, now the only thing connecting them. He used his tongue to wobble the missing tooth's neighbour and after a moment or two, spat that too into the sink. He looked in the mirror again and sadly wished he had taken better care of his teeth when he had the chance. But he hadn't and now they were gone. It was too late. Irretrievable opportunity squandered.

Then he woke up, sweating in the dark. Where was he? The darkness was so thick it almost seemed to have substance. He was lying on something hard, and—oh that's right, he was camping with his friends. He quickly ran his tongue along his teeth—all there. And perfectly solid. No pain. No blood. What a relief. What a freaking relief.

Harold rolled over. He was awake now and likely wouldn't get back to sleep—whenever he had the dream about his teeth falling out he was awake for the rest of the night. It was a recurring dream he'd had ever since his late teens. He'd seen an analyst about it, and the analyst told him it was because he had money worries. Well that was true enough—Harold never had enough money. He lay there trying to think of something to pass the time. He remembered that the next night was his turn to tell an evening ghost story. The thing was, everyone else had already told all the good ones, which were the ones everybody knew anyway— the ghostly hitchhiker, the young couple in the car killed by a psychopath, Bloody Mary, the list went on. Harold realized he was going to have to make up a ghost story of his own, and he was so bored by the idea that he fell asleep.

The next night, Harold and his three friends since high school sat around the campfire. Cassie had been a track and field star, fleet of foot and bright of eye. She had become a corporate headhunter—she always had enough money. Then there was Steve; in high school he'd been a math-whiz, but in adulthood became a high-rise window cleaner because it gave him lots of time to think about abstruse math problems and see things from a different angle. Suzie had been a popular, outgoing girl who was a three-time president of the student council. As a grown-up she'd harnessed her personality and drive to become a well respected mid-level chef—no reality TV shows or bestselling cookbooks, but a good living nonetheless. Finally there was Harold, the bookish kid who had always wanted to be a writer and grew up into a slightly frustrated man who struggled to be a more successful writer than he was, which really oughtn't to have been hard, but was.

All four friends were haunted by doubts and insecurities that gnawed away at them from within. Even the "successful" ones struggled with internal fears and guilt that they shared with no one. Many of these feelings were completely unjustified. Some were merely amplified. Who can say why people feel the way that they do? Whatever the reasons, these four friends were a potent quartet of unresolved feelings and unspoken fears revolving around their own lives—in other words, they were perfectly normal.

Each year, during the late summer, they took leave of their partners, spouses, pets and jobs for a getaway in the woods. And each year, the other three told all the good ghost stories, leaving the dregs for Harold because, after all, he was a writer and ought to be able to come up with something. This year, since they were never satisfied with his stories anyway, Harold had decided simply to make something up on the spot with as little effort as possible.

"Tonight," he began, "I'm going to tell you about the… *klystees*…a group of demons who live in these very woods." Harold had pulled "klystees" out of his head; it just seemed like a scary word. He continued, "You'll never see the klystees or hear them or feel their touch or even smell them, but you'll experience them, for the klystees will latch onto your deepest, grimmest thoughts and cause you to keep thinking them over and over and over again. You'll never be able to break out of the cycle and will be forever doomed to keep thinking those same dreadful thoughts." He looked at the circle of faces around the fire. "*Forever*."

"That's it?" said Cassie.

"Really?" said Steve.

"Worst. Ghost. Story. Ever," said Suzie.

"But then you think the thoughts so long that they become real!" said Harold with an air of desperation.

There was a chorus of "What ev." / "Uh huh." / "Too little, too late." Then they finished eating their marshmallows and retired to their separate tents.

But Harold had done his work better than he knew, for these were the dreams they each had that night.

Cassie, the fleet-footed track-star turned corporate head-hunter, dreamt she was walking peacefully through the woods, the afternoon sunlight falling in shafts through the branches of the trees. Suddenly, behind her, she heard the snap of a twig—without looking she immediately knew that it was a monstrous embodiment of her career as a corporate head-hunter, here to take her own head. Too terrified to turn and look, Cassie started to run but her feet seemed to be stuck in a swamp, and hard as she tried, she couldn't pull away. She struggled and stumbled, taking shorter and slower steps until she could feel the hot breath of the thing on the back of her neck.

But Cassie had had this dream often and knew she was dreaming even as it happened. Usually when the monster was breathing down her neck she would turn around to face it, and just before she was able to bring herself to look at it, she would wake up. Only this time she didn't wake up and turned full round to look into the many eyes of the unspeakable creature intent on taking her head.

Steve's dream was also one that he had had often: he was hanging off the side of a high-rise, cleaning the windows from a scaffold segment suspended by ropes. As his hands automatically went through the motions of applying water to windows and scraping it off with a rubber squeegee blade, Steve's brain was fruitfully engaged in parsing abstract mathematical formulae, thinking about that ground-breaking paper he was going to write some day. When he was finished cleaning the last window, he turned to look out over the city, seeing the patterns of the streets, the flow of the traffic and the paths of pedestrians merge together as proof of the unified theory of life that he was sure was waiting to be discovered—by him.

This was the point in the dream when Steve would realize he'd been so pre-occupied with his formulae and theories that he'd forgotten to secure his safety line. As he moved to tie it off, the rope at one end of the scaffold gave way and, as the scaffold segment dropped suddenly, Steve slid down it, just able to grab a hand-hold at its very end. Now the scaffold segment hung by a single rope, dangling downward with Steve desperately clinging to the lower end. He could feel his grip on the scaffold loosening just as surely as he'd felt his mental grasp of the world expanding. And every time, as he fell through the final moments of the dream, it was with a calm sort of detachment, watching the ground rush up at him with the knowledge that he was dreaming and would wake up before he hit the pavement of the parking lot—but this time, he didn't.

Suzie, the chef, also had a recurring dream. In it, she was for some unexplained reason actually a butcher, not a chef, and was butchering cows, pigs and chickens for consumption by her hungry patrons. But terrifyingly, none of the animals actually seemed to be dead and at the first jab of the knife they would come to life, noisily mooing, oinking or clucking while their severed limbs began to twitch on the cutting board, eventually animating to re-attach themselves to the entirely wrong animal.

And then, in the dream, Suzie would find herself in the forest, desperately running from the odd creatures that pursued her. Now they were joined by the real-life carnivores of the woods—wolves and coyotes, baying and barking for her blood, raging to devour her just as she and her patrons had devoured so many helpless creatures. Each time she had the dream she would feel a sharp nip at her heels as she ran—then another and another. Finally she would feel a sudden weight on her back and then the paws of a wolf pushing her down, bringing her to the ground. And then she would turn her head to see the slavering jaws of the wolf descending toward her face, and then blackness as the gaping maw completely covered her eyes, nose and mouth. Usually it was here that she awoke, but this time, as with her companions, she did not.

When none of them returned from the camping trip, search parties were duly sent out. The searchers didn't have much trouble finding them, but they were at a loss as to what had actually happened. There was no sign of Cassie's head, and to judge from the tooth marks around the neck and shoulders of her body, the animal that had bitten it off must have been enormous. The medical examiner, who had seen pretty much every kind of animal-related death there was, couldn't think of any creature that would be able to snap off a head with one clean bite.

Likewise, he was at a loss to explain why Steve's corpse showed every sign of having fallen from a great height, when none of the nearby trees was taller than 60 feet and the ground under them was soft. One would expect broken bones and injuries causing death, but not a body that looked like it had fallen from 30 stories up and landed in a paved parking lot.

The marks on Suzie's bones at least made sense—sort of. She had clearly been killed by a large predator, likely a wolf, and then the carcass had been picked clean by scavengers. The puzzling thing was that some of her bones bore scratches of what appeared to be cows' teeth, which was very odd, since one, cows are not carnivores, and two, there weren't any farms for miles.

All they found of Harold were his bloodied teeth. The medical examiner had to send them to Harold's dentist to confirm his identity from dental records. The report came back that, yes, they were Harold's teeth…and he really ought to have taken better care of them.

Grab Bag

Jenna and Brad were anxious to get to their camping spot because they both knew what was going to happen—Brad was going to ask Jenna to marry him. She would say yes, and then for the rest of their lives they would tell the story of their engagement as though it had been a carefully planned (on Brad's part) moment of romantic surprise (on Jenna's part).

In reality though, through none-too-subtle suggestion, Jenna had let Brad know she was getting impatient with the ongoing lack of a proposal. They had, after all, been dating for six years, three of which had been spent living happily, if rather dully, together. Brad was something of a dim bulb, and once he'd finally understood why Jenna was upset, it took several more days for him to feebly begin to suspect that this could also be why she kept leaving sticky notes all over the house with "June 15th" written above a little sketch of an engagement ring. Then once he had figured it out, it took several more days for him to decide, first of all, that he'd go through with it, and second, that he'd better come up with some sort of cheesy plan of how to pop the question. The answer, clearly, was to go camping.

And now, when they were just a few miles from their campground, Brad decided to pull over at a roadside souvenir shop. He was getting cold feet and Jenna was getting hot under the collar. But they both went in and looked around. Like other shops of its kind, it sold predominantly "Indian" souvenirs—moccasins, dream catchers, little totem poles, miniature canoes and teepees made out of browned birchbark, and other such trinkets. It smelled pleasantly of scented porcupine quills and leather.

What set this shop apart was that its proprietor was a real honest-to-goodness shaman, and from the minute Brad and Jenna entered his shop, he had them sized up—she wanted certainty in an uncertain world, and he was afraid of certainty in a world devoid of adventure. It was also highly unlikely that either of them would buy anything, and this irked him somewhat. Using every ounce of his skill, the shaman steered them through the shop, inquired if he could help them, listened to them bicker in whispers, interjected to ask if they had looked at a stick of sage grass here or a leaf-shaped chunk of maple candy there, until finally they were beside the mystery bag bin, which also happened to be beside the cash register.

The mystery bags were nothing to look at—little brown paper lunch bags stapled shut with "Mystery Bag" written in marker over the price: two dollars. The writing in marker reminded Brad of the many sticky notes Jenna had left all over the house. He looked up at the shaman, who returned his gaze evenly.

"Uh…I guess we'll get one of these," said Brad, and pulled two dollars out of his pocket.

"Good day to you," said the shaman. He watched Jenna and Brad leave his shop with the warm feeling he got whenever he planted seeds of come-uppances soon to be.

They pulled into the campsite and before they did anything else, went down to watch the sunset on the lake. Jenna was expecting Brad to pull out a little velvet box right there and then and get down on one knee, but he didn't—he just stood there with his arm around her, looking out at the setting sun. And then, after supper, sitting beside the fire, he fished out the brown paper mystery bag, tore it open and held it out to her.

Jenna could barely contain herself—clearly he'd doctored the bag open then hidden the ring in there and stapled it shut. She reached her hand into the bag with every expectation of pulling it out an engaged woman; instead she frowned, fished around and pulled her hand out, cupping... three plastic flies? She looked at the gag flies in her palm. They were just like the ones her brothers used to buy to freeze into ice cubes as practical jokes. She looked up at Brad but he was already fishing around in the bag. He pulled out a little wooden carving of a wolf.

"Your turn again," he said cheerily and obliviously, holding the bag out to her. She stuck her hand in and pulled out the last remaining article: a little metal skull and crossbones. She looked at the flies in one hand and the skull and crossbones in the other and then up at Brad with every ounce of withering contempt she could muster.

"What?" said Brad, and then, putting two and two together, "Oh..."

She flung the plastic flies into the nearby woods and then threw the metal skull and crossbones after them with considerable force. Then she stormed into the tent and huffily got into her sleeping bag.

Brad knew he'd messed up. He sadly tossed the little wolf into the fire and stood up, trying to figure out where he was going to sleep.

The next morning Jenna was feeling a bit more forgiving—after all, today was June 15th—yesterday had only been the 14th—what was she thinking? She felt even more conciliatory when she saw Brad awkwardly trying to sleep on one of the big logs that served as benches around the campfire; he had suffered his well-deserved punishment and it was time for forgiveness. She went and gently prodded his shoulder. He rolled off, shlumped onto the ground, woke up and blearily got to his feet.

"Brad, I just wanted to say, I'm sorry about—" Her words stopped abruptly as she stared at one of the other log benches. On it, neatly lined up, were *the plastic flies, the wooden wolf and the metal skull and crossbones.*

Brad frowned as he followed her gaze and saw the souvenirs himself. Sometimes he did a bit of sleepwalking—they both knew this—he must have gotten up in the night, scoured the woods and found the little treasures, though he was pretty certain he had thrown the wolf into fire the night before.

Jenna reacted calmly. Brad was surprised.

"Okay," said Jenna, edging around to the log with the row of items on it, "we're just going to get rid of these now." She scooped up the plastic flies and before Brad knew what was happening, a dense black cloud of real, live, buzzing black flies had materialized around Jenna! She screamed and doubled over, her face, hands and clothes no longer visible. From head to toe Jenna was wrapped in a writhing cocoon of flies.

Brad did the only thing he could think of. He picked her up, ran down to the shore and threw her into the lake. Instantly the flies vanished and he fished a sputtering, hysterical Jenna out of the water. She didn't have a single bite on her.

Back at the campsite she changed into some dry clothes while Brad lit a fire. When she came out of the tent, she pointed to the remaining souvenirs and said, "I would like you to please get rid of that stuff."

"Sure," said Brad. He went over and picked up the little wooden wolf. In an instant the sky and the very air around them seemed to grow dark. The morning sun was replaced by a full moon, and off in the distance a wolf howled.

"What is going on?" Jenna whimpered. Brad too, as was his lot in life, was baffled.

And now, out of the shadows surrounding the flickering fire, glowing eyes began to emerge, and then a low rumbling growl as the wolf pack materialized out of the darkness all around them. The wolves stalked around the edge of the fire's glow, turning their heads toward Brad and Jenna, keeping an eye on them as they circled ever closer.

"Get rid of that thing!" Jenna screamed, pointing at Brad's clenched hand.

For the second time, he threw the little wooden wolf into the fire and instantly it was morning once more. The fire crackled peacefully. The birds sang in the trees. There were no wolves.

Jenna pointed a trembling finger at the metal skull and crossbones still sitting on the log. "Don't touch that, but get rid of it please. Throw it in the lake."

Using a stick, Brad tipped the little metal skull and crossbones into the brown paper bag the souvenirs had come in. Then with Jenna watching him like a hawk, he walked down to the shore, crumpled up the bag and flung it with all his might out into the water. It landed with a plop and floated there for a few minutes because of the air in the bag, but then sank gradually out of sight.

Back at the campsite, they made breakfast, did the dishes and then doused the campfire. Then they decided to go for a walk to calm down a bit. While Jenna was bustling around getting ready, Brad checked to see that he had the ring. Yes, here was the little red velvet box, and yup, there was the ring, safely inside. He tucked the box into his pants pocket.

He wouldn't do it on the walk but would wait until they returned.

It was a truly relaxing walk. The weather was warm and bright; a casual observer could be forgiven for assuming that Jenna and Brad were warm and bright as well. They walked along, hand-in-hand, not saying much, just enjoying their surroundings. By the time they turned around to head back, Jenna was beside herself—she could tell it was going to happen either on the way or once they were back at the campsite. Brad could tell she knew what was coming and picked up on her excitement.

Back at the campsite, both knew that the moment had finally arrived. Brad seated Jenna firmly on one of the big log benches. Then he got down on one knee in front of her. Then he had to get up again to fumble the red velvet box out of his pocket. Then he got down on one knee again. Jenna's face had gone red and her heart was pounding. It was at this point that Brad noticed, sitting on the log on either side of Jenna, the plastic flies and the wooden wolf. Hmm, that was strange. Good thing Jenna hadn't seen them. Well, he'd get proposed and all that and then they'd get the hell out of there—fast.

"Jenna," he said, "will you marry me?" And with that he opened the box so she could see the ring.

Brad would never forget what happened next. Jenna looked down at the box, screamed, screamed some more, and kept screaming as she ran to the car, got in, started it and drove off, leaving Brad open-mouthed in a cloud of dust. He hadn't seen that coming, but then again he didn't see most things in life coming. He looked down at the box and there, where the ring should have been, was the little metal skull and cross bones.

From the window of the souvenir shop, the shaman smiled as Jenna's car sped past on the highway. A couple of hours later, Brad stumbled by, his thumb raised to passing traffic in the hitchhiker's salute. The shaman smiled again. Brad and Jenna had been luckier than the other ones—they were leaving separately and were unlikely to follow through with their misbegotten vows. They really weren't suited to each other, and now, perhaps, they would see this and find others with whom they could truly live in harmony.

Le Maudite (The Damned)

For 300 years the voyageurs had been paddling. Not a leisurely paddle through the afterlife either, but rather, three centuries at 60 strokes per minute—the frantic pace that had made them famous as *les hommes du nord* (men of the north), capable of almost superhuman exertion as they conquered wood and stream with canoes full of valuable fur pelts. But even ghosts get tired, and now, after hundreds of years, the spectral crew of voyageurs had had about enough.

It had all started in December 1710. This band of hardy paddlers had found themselves deep inland and desperate to get home to their sweethearts for Christmas. But Lachine, their final destination, was hundreds of miles away, and everyone had their doubts that they could make it in time. Jean Baptiste, the senior among them, put on a brave face. "We'll make it yet," he would say. "We'll make it yet, *mes amis*!"

But one night around the fire, Paul LaCroix, a good paddler but a pessimist, piped up with, "*Tabarnak*! We'll never make it home for Christmas and I will not see my sweet Lisette."

"Quit your swearing, Paul LaCroix!" snapped André St. Pierre, crossing himself hurriedly. André was the most pious among them—he had few friends on the shore and even fewer in the little band of voyageurs. "Your *sacrés* will make damned souls out of us all!"

Just then, with a deep pop of hot air and sparks, there appeared, standing in the fire, a beautiful woman.

"Lisette!" cried Paul LaCroix.

"Amelie!" shouted Jacques LaPlante.

"Therese!" rasped François DeVille.

The beautiful woman, her eyes sparkling amorously at all of the men, seemed to face each one at the same time. "I have many names," she said.

"*Mon Dieu*," gasped André St. Pierre, crossing himself again.

"That is not one of them," said the woman slyly.

And now Jean Baptiste saw who, or what, she truly was, for just as the other men saw their sweethearts in her face, he saw, flickering voluptuously in the flames, the curves of his own Clothilde, whom he knew to be waiting for him back in Lachine.

"Be off with you!" Baptiste said defiantly.

"But Jean," said Clothilde's voice from those devilishly full lips, "wouldn't you rather be at home, in my arms right now?"

"*Tabarnak*!" said Paul LaCroix again, though whether from shock or lust was uncertain.

"You all know my name, so we shall not speak it," said the woman. "But I am here to make you an offer: I can see to it that you all get home in time for Christmas, home to the charms of those you most desire."

"My greatest desire is to say a prayer in the cathedral at Montreal," said André St. Pierre.

"But your fellow *hivernants* may not feel the same way," purred the temptress in the flames.

"What would we have to give you in exchange?" spoke up Jean Baptiste, ever clear-headed, but now aching for the caress of Clothilde.

"Why, nothing," said the vision coquettishly. "Unless, of course, one of you should swear during the journey. Then, I am afraid, you will be doomed to paddle the skies for the rest of your unnatural existences."

"*Tabarnak*!" exclaimed Paul LaCroix again.

"That is what I mean," said the sultry apparition, who by this time could be accurately described as both smoking and hot. "If one of you should so much as whisper a little *sacré* then your souls shall paddle their way through eternity."

"All in favour?" asked Jean Baptiste, rounding on the rest of the crew.

Except for the hand of André St. Pierre, which stayed noticeably low, the rest of the crew raised their arms with breathtaking speed.

And so it was done. Before they knew it, the voyageurs found themselves paddling home—not along the waterways they had come by—through the skies, brushing the tree tops! They made good time too, flying at a speed that would have been the envy of any bush-pilot (had they known what bush-pilots were). Even the pious André St. Pierre seemed impressed, though he said nothing, just kept his head down and bent to his paddling.

They paddled through the night, flying over sleeping villages, whisking through the darkened skies until at last the sun began to spill over the horizon, casting beautiful crimson and orange shadows as it spread over the landscape. None of the men had ever seen anything like it before.

"*Tabarnak*!" said Paul LaCroix without even thinking about it.

With a sudden poof the sultry woman of the night before appeared in the sky next to the canoe.

"Well, that's it, *mes amis*," she said archly. "Now you're doomed to paddle the skies for the rest of eternity. Unless, of course, you can find an equal number of mortals to change places with you—good luck with that." And she was gone.

Now cursed anyway, all of the men swore a blue streak at Paul LaCroix—even André St. Pierre. Then, having nothing better to do, they started paddling. For the next 300 years they paddled, watching the world change below them, unable to set foot upon it, unable to stop. They watched as the fur trade dried up. They watched as shining twin lines of railway track joined the country coast to coast. They saw the gradual outgrowth of grey ribbons of road and little darting horseless carriages that effortlessly rolled along those roads. And all the while, they were stuck in the skies, paddling at 60 strokes a minute, wanting to stop and participate in the world "down there" as they came to call it, yearning to take part in all the advances they saw, aching to rejoin a world that seemed to offer so much more than this endless paddling, travelling nowhere fast.

One night as they were skimming across the surface of a moonlit lake, paddling furiously but making no noise, they came suddenly upon a trio of canoes full of campers out for a nighttime paddle. They circled for a moment, listening in on the conversation.

"I'd give anything not to go back to work on Monday," said one of the people. "If I have to sit at that computer for another week, I think my soul will start to rot."

"I know what you mean," said another one. "Doing the same thing day after day after day is so tedious. I wish we could just stay out here and paddle around, forever."

With that, Jean Baptiste had heard enough. As he had been his crew's leader in life, so was he their spokesman in the afterlife. He had observed that their numbers were equal—there were just as many campers as ghostly voyageurs. And so, the ghostly voyageurs now made themselves visible to the campers. Once the initial surprise wore off, the campers agreed to the proposed switch with little or no argument—they would change places. The campers would now paddle the skies at 60 strokes a minute for eternity, while the voyageurs settled into the jobs and lives of the campers. And so, just as quickly as the deal had been made 300 years before, the new deal was struck and concluded and the two parties went their separate ways.

At first, there were the expected growing pains. The voyageurs had been able to observe the passing centuries, but getting used to electricity, learning how to drive, how to do up a zipper, how to read and write, how to use a computer—all of this took time. But then again, the voyageurs still had eternity in front of them. And soon, their blunt, tough labourer's hands were navigating keyboards instead of rivers, and they got used to sitting in swivel chairs instead of kneeling in the bottom of a birchbark canoe.

The hardest thing, though, was that the crew of paddlers effectively had to break up—in the course of a few hours they had gone from being with each other every minute for three centuries to being truly apart—and it was hard. At the beginning, they all enjoyed their new-found solitude. It was also nice to sleep in a soft bed to soothe 300 years' worth of sore paddling muscles. And certainly, spending one's days sitting at a desk was far less gruelling than paddling at 60 strokes a minute.

But one day, Jean Baptiste looked up from his keyboard and realized that he had been typing at 60 words a minute for, well, for as long as he could remember. He looked around at the drab office and suddenly missed his companions, missed soaring over the tree tops, missed seeing the sunrise every morning. Of course it had been tedious paddling all the time and never being able to stop to eat or rest or just enjoy life, but hadn't it been better than this? And he missed his crew—Paul LaCroix's constant swearing and even André St. Pierre's tiresome piety. Now, as he sat alone at his desk in an office full of people and pretty girls who would never understand him, Jean Baptiste saw his future stretching endlessly before him—and wept.

Strong Hands and Squinting Eye

Ben and Mary had been hiking all day when they finally decided to pitch camp in a little forest clearing, surrounded by towering pine trees. The two of them had come on the camping trip because they thought that spending a bit of time alone together might help their relationship, which had been going through a rough patch. They silently built a fire, got supper ready and then washed up their tin cups and plates in the nearby brook. As dusk began to settle, Ben spoke for the first time since they had left their car that morning.

"I know we brought the tent," he said, "but we could just sleep on the ground—under the stars."

"Under the stars and in the bugs," said Mary tiredly.

"There aren't any bugs," replied Ben gently.

Mary raised her eyebrows, shrugged and then actually smiled a weary little grin and nodded. Both of their hearts lifted slightly. They lay side-by-each in their sleeping bags, looking up at the milky way and holding hands. They still didn't speak—there still didn't seem to be anything to say. Presently, they drifted off to their separate, dreamless sleeps.

Mary awoke with a start and leaned over to shake Ben's shoulder. "Do you feel that?" she asked breathlessly.

"Of course I do—you're shaking my shoulder," said Ben sleepily.

"No, not that," said Mary. "It feels like—"

"—the earth is moving!" said Ben, sitting bolt upright in his sleeping bag.

"Do you think it's an earthquake?" asked Mary, huddling a bit closer.

"I don't know what it is," said Ben, standing up in his sleeping bag and pulling Mary up with him in hers. The two of them took a couple of hops backward and then stood there in the moonlight, in their sleeping bags, looking as though they had just hopped across the finish line at a picnic sack-race. And then, there in the little forest clearing, their jaws dropped as two glowing green skeletons clawed their way up from the earth in the very spot they had been sleeping!

After a good deal of unsteady scrabbling and rickety manoeuvring, the two skeletons stood before Ben and Mary, bathing the couple in their sickly aura. Although they didn't know it, for the first time in months, Ben and Mary thought exactly the same thing: "So this is how it ends—like a bad horror movie, and we are the squabbling couple who are the first to die. I wonder how fast we can hop in these sleeping bags."

But just as Ben and Mary had steeled themselves to meet their pointless if improbable deaths, the two skeletons seemed to catch sight of one another and promptly began attacking each other!

First, the skeleton on the left punched the skeleton on the right so hard that Righty's skull spun around, and Righty had to reach up and stop it. Then, in retaliation, Righty ripped off one of Lefty's arms and smacked Lefty's skull clear off of Lefty's shoulders, whereupon it slammed into a tree and started wobbling about on the ground, as though looking for its body. The rest of Lefty's skeleton, now unable to see (on account of not having a head anymore) blindly flailed about until its arm located its adversary and began pummelling Righty until the two skeletons were completely tangled up in one another, a hopeless jumble of interlocked ribs, femurs and ulnas, panting and rattling from their exertions.

Ben and Mary stepped out of their sleeping bags and moved closer to the skeletons. Summoning her courage, Mary walked over to Lefty's wobbling skull and picked it up.

"Hey!" said Lefty's skull in a deep female voice.

"Ah!" shrieked Mary, dropping Lefty's skull.

"Ouch!" said Lefty's skull from down at Mary's feet. "If you're going to pick me up and give me a start then don't drop me right after."

"Er…sorry?" said Mary tentatively.

"Hey, Squinting Eye," called Lefty's skull, "they have manners!"

"That's great, Strong Hands," said Righty. "I wish I could say the same for you." The skeletons briefly resumed their struggle but quickly ceased because they were so constricted by one another that neither one could really move.

Ben and Mary had a quick confab in the middle of the clearing.

"I think the one with the skull is called Squinting Eye," said Mary.

"And the one without the skull's name is Strong Hands," said Ben.

"Hey," called Squinting Eye over to Strong Hands' skull, "they know our names."

Ben and Mary helped Strong Hands and Squinting Eye to disentangle themselves and reattached Strong Hands' skull. Then they lit the campfire, and all four sat around it. Ben and Mary listened as Strong Hands and Squinting Eye told their story.

"Long ago," began Strong Hands in her deep voice, "we had flesh on our bones and we were in love with each other, just as you are now." Ben and Mary glanced at one another uncomfortably.

"But then," continued Squinting Eye, "we began to bicker—just as you do now." Another uncomfortable glance between the living followed this barbed comment from the dead.

"What did you bicker about?" asked Ben.

"What does anyone bicker about?" replied Strong Hands, grinding her head back to the night sky and giving every impression of rolling her eyes, even though she didn't have any.

"We lived in a village on the other side of the river," said Squinting Eye. "And if you want to know why we bicker, you have only to consider our names. I was called Squinting Eye because I had a knack for peering ahead to see how the future might unfold. Even if the summer was fertile, I could foresee that the winter would be a hard one. If two friends quarrelled I could suggest ways that, given time, might mend the friendship. It wasn't anything supernatural—through years of practice, I just had a knack for seeing the direction events could take and took appropriate actions to prepare."

"And I was known as Strong Hands because I was a champion huntress and my bow was so large that I was the only one strong enough to draw it. I wrestled bears, mountain lions and wolverines, and always, I was the one who returned with their pelts slung over my shoulder. My strength was not just in my hands but in my generous spirit as well, for our entire village knew they could depend on my prowess when times were lean. As a couple, the entire village looked to us for support and guidance."

"But," said Squinting Eye, "we argued."

"Why?" Mary wanted to know.

"Because Squinting Eye here," said Strong Hands, "was always squinting his eyes at me, warning me off of a certain course of action, never letting me just live in the present, always with an eye to the consequences."

"Because there *are* consequences," said Squinting Eye. "Whenever there was a potlatch so that those in need could take what they required, you wanted to give away everything we had!"

"Because I knew I could always get more!" rumbled Strong Hands ominously.

"And I knew that there were tough times approaching and that we wanted to start a family!" cried Squinting Eye with a haunting note of anguish in his voice.

There was silence for a few minutes.

"Then what happened?" asked Ben.

"Well," said Strong Hands wearily, "our village began to suffer for our disagreements and one night, Manitou, the Great Spirit, appeared to us and said, 'Your arguments are so loud that not only do they threaten the harmony of your village, but they also drown out my drumming. You know I like to drum, and when my drumming cannot be heard all of nature falls into disharmony. Squinting Eye, you must learn to see the present for more than the impact it will have on the future. And Strong Hands, you must resist the urge to give away all you have gathered even for the sake of others—your generosity is wasted if you dispense it all in one place. You both must mend your ways, lest the worst of all fates befalls you.' And with that, the Great Spirit Manitou vanished."

"Did you listen his advice?" asked Mary.

"We're a couple of glowing green skeletons," said Strong Hands. "What do you think?"

"We did not heed Manitou's words," said Squinting Eye sadly. "We continued to argue and slowly, the others in our village drifted away to new places. Then there was a harsh winter and one day, Strong Hands was preparing to go hunting since we had given all of our food to the others to take on their journeys. However, I could see that there was a blizzard blowing in and I warned Strong Hands that she might perish if she left our shelter. Uncharacteristically, she obeyed me and so we had no food and we starved to death, lying in side-by-each. Slowly the winds blew down our shelter, blew the sands of the earth over our bodies and laid us to rest as peacefully as possible."

"But Manitou had other plans for us," said Strong Hands. "During our long sleep that winter, he came to us and told us that we would slumber in the earth until we were awakened by those who might help us solve our differences."

"And that's us?" asked Ben.

Neither of the skeletons said anything. In fact, none of them said anything for several minutes. Presently, Mary asked in a quiet voice, "Squinting Eye, with your gift for seeing how things might turn out, couldn't you foresee what might happen if you and Strong Hands continued in your ways?"

The skeleton that had been Squinting Eye sighed rustily. "I could not."

Then Ben asked, "Strong Hands, with your great strength and generosity of spirit, couldn't you see the virtue of being generous to yourself and Squinting Eye?"

The former Strong Hands heaved a great, rattling sob. "I could not."

But Squinting Eye stomped on her grief, suddenly angry again. "That's right, you could give and give to everyone else, but just not to me or us or our future together!"

"I see!" said Strong Hands. "So nothing has changed for you—always the future, the future, the future, never the present."

And with that the two glowing skeletons stood up and Strong Hands lived up to her name by striking Squinting Eye's skull clean off his shoulders. The rest of Squinting Eye ran over to his skull, picked it up with both hands and ran off through the woods followed in hot pursuit by Strong Hands, each of the skeletons bellowing at the top of their ghostly voices. Ben and Mary watched as the two restless spirits faded into the distance, running toward the future, away from the present and, in so many ways, back into their shared past.

The young couple sat quietly, now truly understanding what it was to be haunted—not by glowing green skeletons, but by the idea of two people unable to solve their differences, by the idea of what would happen if they kept on as they were, by the idea that understanding future consequences wasn't always enough to inspire sensible actions in the present. And then, Ben and Mary lay down again in their sleeping bags, looking up at the stars, neither one finding the words they felt as though they ought to say.

GPS

There were only three of them in the *GPS* crew. Katee was the producer-director, shaping the story as they went. Liam was the camera operator. Wyatt was the sound recordist. In this case, "GPS" stood not for "global positioning system," the device that so many drivers use to find their way around, but rather *Ghostly Phenomena Searchers*, the name of the TV show they were filming.

For this week's episode, working title "Runners of Death," the researchers had dug up a man named Frank Westmacott, a fifty-something with an ancient crumbling diary that recounted a journey from the early 1700s. Two greedy fur traders—*coureur de bois* or "runners of the woods"—had turned on a third and tortured him into revealing the location at which he had cached a hoard of silver coins that were to be used to pay Indian trappers for their furs. But, mistrustful of their victim, the two villains of the piece then dragged him along to show them the way. None of the three men had ever returned, but it was a family legend that the diary had mysteriously turned up one day on the doorstep of one of Frank Westmacott's ancestors.

And now the little band of modern-day adventurers was deep in the woods trying to follow the tangled directions of Frank's ancestor, who had almost certainly been a murderer. They were hoping for a sighting of the so-called Deepwood Ghost, a glowing figure that witnesses occasionally observed flitting through the trees deep in the heart of the forest. It was rumoured to be the spirit of Gilles Desmarais, the victim of Hamish Westmacott and the other greedy trader, Thomas Ludgate.

On this, their first night in the woods, Wyatt and Liam were bored—they'd been on dozens of these shoots and there were never any ghosts, just shadows and sounds that Katee and the guest "expert" would use to try to convince each other that they'd captured some sort of spirit manifestation on video. For her part, Katee just wanted to get a spooky story, which shouldn't be hard out in the woods at nighttime. Frank was the only one who seemed worried—he felt bad about his ancestor's part in the presumed murder of Gilles Desmarais. At the very least he wanted to acknowledge and publicly accept the fact that his ancestor had killed a man.

Frank and Katee were pouring over the diary. It didn't have traditional longitude and latitude notations, but rather a confusing maze of directions such as "two minutes North; 30 seconds North north east; 45 seconds East north east," and so on. But Katee and Frank had patiently tried to follow the directions and now, as far as they could tell, they were at the spot where Gilles Desmarais had briefly escaped his captors and fled into the woods. But, oddly, instead of trying to actually get away, he had apparently spent several minutes arranging scores of fist-sized stones to spell out "*Tu es mort*"—French for "You are dead."

As Hamish Westmacott's diary said, "When we found the dog and his vain message, we hefted one of the rocks out of the word 'Tu' and used it to bludgeon him about the head and shoulders a bit, not putting an end to him, but teaching him a lesson."

Frank winced as he read that part and then suddenly looked up. "What was that?" he said in a low voice. "I'm sure I just saw something."

Katee looked at Liam and Wyatt. They both sighed and picked up the camera and microphone.

"I'm sure a just saw a glowing figure walking through the trees," said Frank. "Look! There!"

Liam and Wyatt were busy readying the camera and sound equipment and missed seeing whatever it was. Katee thought that she might have seen some sort of glowing flash, but it could have been fireflies. The four of them stood there in the dark, the camera running, but no glowing figure emerged from the trees.

Finally Katee said, "Well, turn on the light on the camera. We might as well go poke around in the woods to show that we investigated." The little group pushed through the darkened trees, following the intense beam of the light mounted on top of the camera. Suddenly, Liam tripped on something and the camera jarred. He aimed the light down so they could all see.

There, freshly laid out, not covered by earth and leaves as they would be if they had been there for 300 years, were scores of fist-sized stones spelling out "*Tu es mort.*" There was a stone missing from the "T" in "Tu."

After a restless night with one of them taking watch every couple of hours, the four arose, had breakfast and pushed on. Their goal today was to find the site of the so-called "false-dig," the point at which Gilles Desmarais had sworn he had buried his hoard of silver coins, but where determined digging 300 years earlier had yielded nothing. As the diary said, "The dog Desmarais led us to a spot and swore that here his hoard was buried. We forced him to dig but no silver was found. We took the shovel and bloodied him considerably, whereupon he admitted that the true treasure site was some miles onward."

Following the confusing directions in the diary, the four of them had at last arrived at a spot that seemed to match the description in the diary, just at the crook of a little nearby stream.

"Okay," said Katee. "We're going to get some footage of you digging here, Frank, and then Wyatt and Liam will take over to really dig out a hole."

"Why are we even digging here at all?" asked Liam indignantly. "We know there's no treasure here."

"Yeah," said Wyatt. "Especially when we know the last page of the diary is torn out, and we'll never know where the treasure is or what really happened."

"You just don't want to dig," said Katee.

"And there's that," said Wyatt.

Frank said, "Look guys, I'll help you dig. I really want to get to the bottom of this. And don't forget about the weird symbol in the back of the diary—if we can figure out what that means then that could give us a clue." Frank gingerly turned the pages of the diary until he got to the words "Dig here" written over an odd trio of symbols: a triangle, a circle and then another triangle.

Sullenly, Liam and Wyatt taped Frank beginning to dig and then put down the equipment and joined him. The morning wore on and by mid afternoon, they'd dug down to about six feet when Katee suddenly said, "Did one of you cut yourselves?"

The three men looked up at her from the bottom of the pit and then at themselves—sure enough, they were all covered in speckles of what looked like blood.

"Look," said Wyatt. "It's seeping in from the sides of the hole." And even as they watched, the little rivulets of red that were flowing down the sides of the hole turned into a bloody torrent. The three men scrambled to get out of the hole, clawing their way up the sides until they emerged and stood, each covered in crimson.

By the time they came back from washing up in the stream and changing into clean clothes, the hole was full of blood. At Katee's urging they picked up the equipment and shot some footage of the gory hole, Frank briefly explaining what had happened for the benefit of the camera.

That night they all saw the glowing figure, darting through the trees like a fugitive spirit. They were prepared this time, with camera and sound at the ready. It darted and ducked so quickly that they couldn't be sure of what it was doing.

The next day, when they reviewed the footage, they saw that the ghostly silhouette seemed to be pointing, gesturing for them to go east—and so they did. As they walked, Wyatt wondered aloud, "Why should this Gilles Desmarais character want to haunt the woods anyway?"

"Well," said Frank, "to keep anyone else from getting the treasure that he died to save."

"If that's the case, why is his ghost showing us the way to go?" asked Liam.

"Good question," said Frank.

"And why should he spell out a message in stones to tell us we're dead and then fill up a hole with blood?"

"Also a good question," said Frank.

"Maybe he wants his story to finally be told," chimed in Katee.

Wyatt, Liam and Frank rolled their eyes and kept trudging onward. An overcast morning had turned into a gloomy afternoon by the time they stopped for a meal break by a large pond that seemed to be perfectly circular. In the distance, two rocky hills loomed up like guarding sentinels.

Katee was just thinking that the pond in the foreground and the mountains in the background would make a great shot when it struck her. "Hey," she said, "this is it! This is where we're supposed to dig!"

"What do you mean?" Frank asked.

"Look at the symbols in the back of the diary."

Frank flipped it open and they all clustered around to look at the little drawing that showed a circle between two triangles.

"It's those two rocky hills and this pond lined up in the foreground between them," she said breathlessly.

"I think you're right," said Frank.

This time they all started digging, even Katee. They kept a steady pace going, Wyatt and Liam occasionally stopping to shoot some footage. Abruptly, Katee pointed to something on Wyatt's shovel and said, "Is that a bone?"

Sure enough it was. Gingerly they uncovered a skeleton lying in the earth. And then, over the next hour, a *second* one lying beside the first. By this time the sun was sinking behind the hills, the blue veil of dusk rising up all around them.

"Why are there two skeletons?" asked Liam.

"I've been thinking about that," said Wyatt, turning to Frank. "You're the expert on this. Has anyone ever considered the possibility that Gilles Desmarais led his captors to the treasure's hiding place, dug it up and then somehow overpowered them and killed them, then took his treasure and went off to start a new life?"

"As far as I know, you're the first person to suggest that," said Frank.

Liam and Wyatt got the camera ready in case there were more sightings of the glowing figure now that it was dark.

Eventually, they saw a shimmering blip far off in the woods and now, for the first time, a second glowing figure also became visible. Both silhouettes were darting in and out of the trees, but drawing rapidly closer to where the little group stood.

"So," said Katee. "That would mean that the Deepwood Ghost is actually two ghosts, the ghosts of the Hamish Westmacott and Thomas Ludgate."

"That's right," said Frank for the benefit of the camera, as the two shimmering spectres advanced quickly. "The ghost of my ancestor and his ghastly partner—two angry men with homicidal tendencies."

"So we're stuck in the middle of nowhere with a couple of angry ghosts?" said Wyatt.

When the *GPS* crew didn't report back to the city, search parties were duly sent out. Eventually, beside the circular pond with the rocky hills in the distance, the searchers found the camera, the sound equipment and all of the tapes, but there was no sign of Katee, Liam, Wyatt or Frank. When they reviewed the tapes and pieced the story together, they were puzzled; despite the crew clearly believing they had captured a glowing figure (or figures) on the tapes, there were none to be seen. And even more puzzlingly, despite the fact that the tapes showed all four members of the expedition digging a large hole by the pond, upon examination of the actual site, no signs of digging could be found, much less the large hole that ought to have been there.

Out of deference to the next of kin, the episode was never aired.

2
Ghosts in the
Modern World

The Picture of Doreen Gray

Doreen Gray was "a woman of a certain age," as the old saying goes. Really, it just meant that, in her own mind, she was too old to meet a man. She thought of herself as a carton of milk whose "best before" date long since passed. It wasn't true, but it was just the way she thought.

She had also lurched through life with a succession of jobs instead of a career. She often wondered if perhaps she ought to make some sort of plan for the future, but living day to day, job to job, paycheque to paycheque was just so much more fun. Besides, focusing on something, really concentrating, was just so hard and tedious. Better to go down the path of least resistance as a flirty dead-end jobber than embark on the considerably more difficult path of actually trying. She envied her friends their stability and relationships, but not the staid predictability of their days.

Finally though, into every life a little rain must fall, or at least a sliver of reality intrude. In Doreen's case it was the morning she looked into the mirror and saw someone who looked…old. The laugh lines at the corners of her eyes were starting to become crow's feet. Her once smooth forehead was furrowed with the worry of a day-to-day existence. The skin under her chin seemed just a little looser than it had the day before. She got a sudden and unpleasant sensation of time slipping away.

So, she decided to try online dating. Then she realized that to try online dating, she'd need to know how to use a computer. And then she realized that maybe she should

take a course in how to do that. She went down to the local
community college and signed up for one.

She hadn't been in a classroom since high school, and she
was relieved to see that she wasn't the oldest one there—not
by far. And the teacher was so cute! He probably thought she
was too old for him, but he was still nice to look at.

To Doreen's surprise, she liked learning something new.
It was an introductory course that covered the basics: "word
processing" (or as Doreen thought of it, typing) and a bit
about working with "digital images" (or as Doreen thought
of them, photos on the computer).

Through all of it, the cute instructor's constant refrain
was to "back up" your work, which meant saving copies of
things you were working on so that you'd have a spare if
something went wrong—Doreen wasn't so interested in that
part. What she was interested in was what you could do to
a photo on the computer. If it was colour you could make it
black and white. If it was too dark, you could make it a bit
lighter. And if you had crow's feet at the edges of your eyes,
you could erase them.

Once the course was done Doreen went down to the
computer store and bought a used laptop that, unbeknownst
to her, was haunted by the unhappy spirit of its previous
owner. Then she got the guy at the store to set the computer
up for her and went home to start meeting people on the
Internet.

First, though, she needed to do a bit of work on the picture of herself that she was going to put up on the dating
website. Feeling very virtuous, she heeded her instructor's
advice to back up; she took a photo of herself, loaded it on
the computer, saved it, then made a copy of it. On the copy,
she went to work—she took away the pleasant-looking

crow's feet at the corners of her eyes and smoothed out a couple of other wrinkles that lent her face character but not youth. It definitely made her look younger.

The next morning she shuffled out of bed and looked in the mirror with the vague sense of dread that had become part of her morning routine. But this time, she had to look twice—it looked as though her crow's feet were a little less... crow's footish, and her other wrinkles seemed less noticeable. She decided it was probably just in her mind since she felt good about putting up her online dating profile. Speaking of which, it was time to see if anyone was interested. She went to the dating website and saw that someone was asking her out for that night. She clicked to say yes.

Her date turned out to be a guy called Bill who was an insurance claims adjuster. He was about her age, and the evening seemed to be going well until Bill asked what Doreen did for a living. As she described her nomadic employment history, the glimmer of interest in Bill's eyes seemed to dim. He was very nice about it, but he told her that he wanted to meet someone who was self-sufficient and who was "going somewhere." Bill had a plan for the future, and he wanted a companion who was looking ahead too (the implication being that Doreen wasn't). With that, Bill very nicely paid the bill and made his exit.

Doreen went home in a huff and looked at herself in the mirror. Then she looked at the photo of herself she'd posted on the dating website. After several moments of unaccustomed thought, she decided that all her problems would be solved, not if she got some sort of plan in life, but rather, if she looked younger in her online dating photo.

In the back of her mind she thought about her cute computer instructor's constant warning to "back up. Whatever else you do, back up." But that would mean saving a copy of the photo that she had already made herself look younger in, and she was impatient to begin. Besides, she had saved a copy of the original photo; if anything went wrong, she could start again on that one. Anyway, backing up once was fine, but doing it every time she made a change would be such a pain.

So she went to work, shaving more years off the already younger-looking image of herself. Doreen continued on late into the night, blending away the lines that furrowed her forehead and softening the lines that sagged downward from the corners of her mouth. When she was done, she sat back and admired her handiwork.

"Back up?" she said to herself. "How can you move forward if you're always backing up?" She looked at the new face in the photo with a sense of elation. Surely now she would meet someone who didn't care whether she was a waitress or a window washer. Feeling that she had done a good night's work, she went to bed.

The next morning Doreen rolled out of bed feeling lighter on her feet than she had in years. She loped into the bathroom, looked in the mirror and froze. The wrinkles on her forehead were nearly gone; her brow was as smooth and unwrinkled as it had been 20 years ago. The lines that pulled the corners of her mouth down were gone as well, and now her lips, which were fuller and redder, just as she had made them in the photo, seemed to turn up cheerfully at the ends. Doreen felt as though an icy finger were tracing its way down her spine. She looked down at the rest of herself—was she actually getting thinner and firmer?

She booted up the computer and logged on to her dating profile. A guy named Kevin had asked her out for a drink. She said yes right away. And then she looked at her photo.

Now that she thought about it, there were still some other things she could do to improve her looks—but that would have to wait until later. Right now, she had tables to wait on.

Her date that night with Kevin started out really well. He and Doreen were about the same age, but now she actually looked a few years younger than he did. He was a bank manager, and Doreen thought he was quite handsome. As the evening progressed, it became apparent that Kevin was quite entranced by Doreen; he didn't care if she was a waitress, a window washer or an undertaker—he just liked her. And perhaps that was the problem, for as the evening went on, Doreen started to think that she could do even better now that she had her new looks. Did she really want someone whose life was so predictable? And who looked older than she did? Doreen decided that the answer was no, told Kevin as much and left him to pay the bill.

When she got home, she turned on her computer and looked closely at her photo. Without bothering to save a copy, she started in again, colouring in the grey roots that were still showing in the picture and then tightening up the loose fold of skin under her chin, the last tell-tale clue to her real age. She compared her current photo to her original one; side-by-each, the two photos were a study in contrasts. The original, the "old" Doreen, showed a face that was friendly and attractive, its expression of goodwill more than making up for what it lacked in wisdom. The second photo, the one that she had relentlessly edited, showed a younger, tighter face with the blandly arrogant expression that Doreen had seen staring back from magazine covers at the grocery checkout. This, she told herself, was the "real" Doreen.

The next morning Doreen positively bounded out of bed and into the bathroom to look in the mirror. She looked

20 years younger at least and felt amazingly fit and optimistic. She perched herself on the chair in front of the computer, logged on to her dating site, clicked yes to a request from Tim without even bothering to look at his photo and then left for work, full of anticipation.

That night Doreen headed out to the bar where she was meeting Tim. She walked in and saw, sitting at a table in the corner, her very cute computer instructor.

"Are you Tim?" she asked him, scarcely able to believe her luck.

"I am," said Tim. "And you're Doreen." He looked at her closely, clearly sensing something familiar about her but not actually recalling her from his computer class. She didn't wonder—they looked the same age now—she was a completely new Doreen.

And so they started to talk; they had a lot in common. Tim was tired of living the responsible life of a computer teacher at a community college and wanted to move on to chase his dream of starting his own software company. Doreen barely understood any of it, but got just enough of his drift to understand that he wanted to do something more than what he was doing—something new and exciting that wasn't just the same thing day after day.

But then Tim said something that brought it all crashing down for her: "I know that if it doesn't work out I can always go back to teaching. That's my fall-back, teaching. I tell my students over and over that they should back up their work, and it applies to life too—you've got have a fall-back, a back-up plan."

And with those simple words, Doreen felt old all over again, without a back-up plan, without any sort of plan, still struggling along doing the same old dumb stuff she did every day. And she was angry—angry at Tim for making her *feel* old when she *looked* so young.

Doreen stood up melodramatically and a little unsteadily (she had definitely had too much to drink), then glared down at Tim and slurred, "Well...well...how can you move forward if all you're ever doing is backing up? You'll never go anywhere, my *young friend*." Almost spitting these last words, she spun contemptuously on her heel and stalked out of the bar, leaving a very puzzled and somewhat wounded Tim in her wake.

Doreen stumbled home and slouched in front of the computer. She looked at her photo and looked for something to improve, but there was nothing. As far as Doreen was concerned, she was now perfect. Living in the moment had paid off for her.

But now we come to the unhappy spirit haunting Doreen's computer and orchestrating all of the remarkable changes in her appearance. The ghost had gone along with Doreen's changes to the photo, altering her actual features as she gradually changed the features of her photo. Although it was a mean spirit, it was not entirely evil. In fact, all the ghost wanted to do was to have a bit of fun, giving Doreen false hope by making her appear gradually younger and then reversing the process to slowly and disappointingly age her back to normal. But the ghost found itself stymied— how could it gradually age her again when it had no record of how Doreen had looked at the different stages of her transformation? All the frustrated spirit had to go by was the current photo of the hard, artificially youthful Doreen and the original photo showing her true face and body shape. Throwing up its spectral hands, the ghost decided to just age her back all at once.

Doreen was still in front of the computer admiring her many perfections when a dialogue box popped up on the laptop's screen:

TIME TO FACE REALITY ONCE AGAIN. THIS WOULD HAVE BEEN EASIER IF YOU HAD BACKED UP.

As she read the pop-up message, Doreen's heart started pounding. What had happened? Suddenly she felt unwell and dashed to the bathroom, stopping in front of the mirror. There, in front of her very eyes, all of the wrinkles, creases and imperfections she had so painstakingly erased were quickly reappearing. She could feel them too—she felt the accustomed frown furrow her brow, the skin around her cheeks and mouth felt heavy, the skin under her chin felt flabby, and all over her body 20 years of aches, pains and gradual deterioration reasserted themselves. The miraculous transformation to her younger self had happened gradually over several days and mostly as she slept, but now the sudden change back to reality was too much for her heart and she collapsed, clutching first at her left arm and finally her chest.

Privately most of Doreen's friends shook their heads. To them it looked like, yes, she had finally gotten some sort of plan—she had learned how to use a computer and had joined an online dating site—but it was a plan that was far too late. They didn't say any of that at the funeral though. Just how she enjoyed living for the moment…

The Devil Driver

"Damn this thing!" Darren Pinto cursed under his breath.

Changing the ink cartridges in his computer printer was one of his least favourite activities. It looked easy for everybody else. How many times had Darren watched his friends snap the ink cartridges into place and print something as though nothing had happened? A lot of times, was how many. But whenever Darren tried to do it, either the ink cartridges wouldn't quite snap into place or, even if he got them in, the computer would steadfastly refuse to print.

"Curse this thing!" he swore again.

Finally he got the finicky little ink cartridges properly wedged into their spots and closed the printer cover. Now the printer would print a test page to show that the cartridges were working properly, using all the different colours of ink. Darren also hated this part because, assuming he could get the stupid thing to work, the test page used up at least half of the ink he had just struggled so hard to insert.

He flicked the power switch on the printer and nothing happened. He flicked it on and off again several times and then said, "Dammit!"

As if on cue, the printer wheezed to life. Painfully slowly, the test page inched forward. Darren would usually ignore it until it was complete, then give it a cursory glance to make sure all the wasteful little squiggles of colour had printed properly before throwing the page into his recycling bin. But this time, once the printer had finished, he glanced over at the paper tray and squinted. There didn't seem to be any coloured squiggles on the test page, just a line of tiny print in the middle of the page.

"Great," he said to himself, "the blasted thing has probably printed an error message and I'll have to go through that rigmarole all over again! Damn this printer!"

He went over to the printer, grabbed the test page and read what was printed there:

YOU ARE GOING TO DIE.

Upon reading this, Darren wasn't so much scared as puzzled. How was this possible? Was it some sort of programmer's trick built into the computer or the printer? He fiddled around with the computer and quickly found the menu he was looking for. He clicked "Print Test Page" and stood back to see what came out:

YOU ARE GOING TO DIE HORRIBLY.

And then, before Darren could do anything else, the printer began printing of its own accord and out came another page:

THIS IS NO TRICK.

Hurriedly, Darren shut down the computer, but the printer still slid a new sheet onto the tray:

IT'S NO USE.

Now frantic, Darren unplugged both the computer and the printer. But even with no apparent source of electrical power, the printer slid yet another sheet into its paper tray:

YOU ARE RUNNING LOW ON TONER.

Running low on toner? Well that was ridiculous—he had an inkjet printer that used coloured liquid ink to print.

Toner was a powder—a completely different way of printing. His printer might be possessed, but it clearly didn't know what it was talking about. And then a final sheet slid into the paper tray with a final message:

THIS IS THE END.

And with that, a spinning black whirlwind of toner powder rose up out of the printer like an angry python and forced itself down Darren's throat. His final thought was, *This is impossible.*

Interestingly, "this is impossible" was the very first thought that ran through the minds of Darren's horrified friends when they found him a couple of weeks later, his face, neck and shoulders horribly blackened as though he'd been trapped in a coal mine. His printer was, after all, an inkjet—there was no reason that he should have suffocated on black, powdery toner. There wasn't a toner cartridge to be found anywhere in his entire apartment, and even if there had been, it still wouldn't explain how it had apparently been forced down his throat. His friends (and the police) were also baffled by the six test sheets Darren seemed to have printed, each one covered with identical squiggly coloured lines from his inkjet printer.

Heaven Scent

Brittnee, Selena and Kylie all worked at Amblett's department store. They all dressed identically—sheer black blouses over stretchy black camisoles, with black slacks that were form-fitting at the top and loose at the bottom. They wore black shoes with just enough of a heel not to be sensible. The three of them hovered at or around their sales areas like a trio of black-clad exclamation points. Brittnee worked in lingerie and unmentionables; Selena worked in the women's wear department; and Kylie worked at the cosmetics counter. The three of them were saddened when their comrade in black, Amber, who worked at the fragrance counter, was fired for being too dumb to use the cash register.

They were even more saddened when they saw that Amber's replacement was an angular woman in her sixties named Miss Terwilliger. Instead of dressing all in black, which was store policy, Miss Terwilliger had apparently somehow convinced the management at Amblett's to make an exception in her case—and it was quite an exception. Miss Terwilliger's daily uniform looked as though it would be more at home officiating at a country fair than working in a high-end department store; she wore sensible shoes, a long tweed skirt and a blazer in an oversized red and pink plaid over a frilly blouse. There was a sparkly brooch in the shape of a flower pinned onto her jacket, and she wore her straight grey hair pulled back into a bun. And in contrast to her colleagues' alarm, Miss Terwilliger was quite eager to meet all of them.

"And what do vivacious young women such as yourselves do in your spare time?" asked Miss Terwilliger. "Romance? Adventure?"

"Well," said Brittnee, furrowing her brow, "I really like shopping."

"And I like to go on Facebook all the time and I also like to send text messages to my friends," said Selena. "And I have a little dog."

"I like to watch TV with my boyfriend," said Kylie.

"Excellent," said Miss Terwilliger. "But what are your interests, your leisure time activities? Current affairs? Stamp collecting? Helping the needy?"

None of them really knew what Miss Terwilliger meant, and they were surprised and slightly baffled by the genuine look of sad dismay on her face when she saw that they didn't understand her.

"I keep the shopping bags from all the stores I shop at," said Brittnee uncertainly.

"I take my little dog for walks," said Selena.

"I like to watch TV with my boyfriend," said Kylie.

Miss Terwilliger nodded at them and then, with a distant look in her eye, returned to the fragrance counter.

But, odd and old-fashioned as their new colleague seemed, Brittnee, Selena and Kylie had to admit that she had a way with customers. One day, a teary-eyed young woman came into the store. As she moved from counter to counter, it emerged that she had just been dumped by her boyfriend and was seeking solace through retail therapy. Brittnee tried to interest her in sexy new underwear, but that didn't work. Nor was she interested in the 2-for-1 sale on capri pants in Selena's department, and Kylie's sales pitch for a make-up makeover fell upon indifferent ears. But when the young woman reached Miss Terwilliger's fragrance counter, she stopped. Miss Terwilliger smiled at her and she smiled back. Kylie, who was close by, overheard the conversation.

"Well," said Miss Terwilliger, "I can certainly identify with the heartbreak you're going through. Heaven knows I've been jilted by a paramour or two in my day, abandoned by fickle suitors, passed over by callow youths, misled by cads and all that sort of thing."

The young woman looked slightly puzzled but smiled bravely.

"Now," said Miss Terwilliger, "we're not supposed to do this, but I'm going to mix you up a little fragrance of my own. I know, I know, we're supposed to sell only the brand name scents, but I just find that they smell of alcohol and plastic. I think this one will bring out the high notes in your natural scent and anchor your bass notes for a firm foundation."

And with that, Miss Terwilliger turned away for a moment and Kylie could hear the clink of bottles behind the counter. She was alarmed—this was totally against the rules. Then Miss Terwilliger turned back to her customer and daubed a bit of the scent she'd created onto the young woman's wrist.

Well, that's it, thought Kylie to herself, *Miss Terwilliger has gone too far—that poor girl is crying.*

Indeed the young woman's eyes had filled with tears, but now she was smiling too. "Oh, thank you!" she said to Miss Terwilliger. "I don't know how you've done it, but this reminds of the smell of the playground when I was a kid— sunlight and dust and fun and friendship. I see now that I can still have all that…that I do still have all that. I'll take three bottles, please. Thank you again."

The next day, a woman strode into the store emanating waves of rage, her eyebrows drawn into an angry V-shape. As she made the rounds, it emerged that she had just lost her job, fired to make a spot for someone less qualified but distantly related to the boss. She angrily spurned Brittnee's suggestion that a push-up bra might make her feel better, peevishly frowned at Selena's business casual sale and openly sneered at Kylie's newest celebrity cosmetics line, Vapid: The Paris Hotel Collection. But when she came to Miss Terwilliger's fragrance counter, she stopped and the two women started to chat like a couple of old friends. Selena was curious and wandered over to eavesdrop.

"I know just how you feel," said Miss Terwilliger. "In my day I've been passed over for more promotions than I've got toes and fingers. I've trained others to do my job and then been let go. I've watched as those younger, simpler and less qualified than me were promoted while I remained at my station. Now, we're not supposed to do this, but I'm going to mix you up a little fragrance of my own. We're supposed to sell only the brand name perfumes, but I just find that they all smell like flowers and arrogance."

And with that, Selena watched as Miss Terwilliger turned away and started clinking her bottles together. After a moment's work she turned back to her customer and daubed a bit of the fragrance onto the woman's wrist.

The woman took a sniff and her face broke into a wide smile. "How did you do that? It smells just like the wet concrete when we'd wash my parents' car in the summer. Those were the best days—we'd have water fights with the hose and it felt like the world was waiting, whether it was just around the corner or across the ocean. How did you manage to work all that into such a simple scent?"

"Well," said Miss Terwilliger, "I may not have always been promoted when I thought I should be, but I've learned a thing or two in my travels."

The woman bought several bottles of the scent and left the store considerably happier than when she had arrived.

The day after that another sombre-looking woman came into Amblett's and wondered aimlessly around the store, her eyes glassy and her gait rather hopeless. Brittnee discovered that the woman wasn't looking for anything in particular, but her mother had just passed away and…well, that was all there was to tell, really. Brittnee asked if perhaps the woman would be interested in some new underwear, but received only a listless shake of the head. Selena and Kylie's out-of-place overtures similarly failed.

All three of them lurked to see what Miss Terwilliger would do. It was the usual routine; Miss Terwilliger surreptitiously turned away, clinked her bottles together and, a few moments later, turned back to her grieving customer, took one listless hand in hers and daubed some scent onto the woman's wrist.

Since the woman was already teary, it was difficult to tell what exactly happened next—the woman touched her wrist to her nose and then her shoulders seemed to slump even further. She lowered her head onto the counter for a moment and then stood up, her eyes still wet but a little brighter, and her shoulders square. "It's the smell of turkey dinner at Christmas," she said, looking in amazement at Miss Terwilliger. "The smell of a house full of family and friends—love abounding."

The woman was of course still grieving but now looked as though she once again at least had hope. She bought a single bottle of scent and stepped gingerly out of the store.

After this incident, Brittnee, Selena and Kylie approached Miss Terwilliger and asked her what her secret was.

"It's simple," said Miss Terwilliger. "I'm a ghost. I've been mixing scents since the time of the pharaohs. I've mixed scents for queens and wastrels, kings and beggars. Wherever there are people in distress, I can mix a scent to salve their grief."

Brittnee, Selena and Kylie didn't really believe her, but by sheer coincidence, the next day found all three of them sorely in need of Miss Terwilliger's special knack. Brittnee's favourite clothing store, Sweat Shop International, closed its doors amid harrowing allegations of child labour, which Brittnee neither understood nor cared about. Selena's friends had not communicated with her on Facebook or sent text messages for a whole three hours the day before, and this had left her in quite a state. Meanwhile, Kylie's favourite TV show had been cancelled and she was acutely upset. All three girls were in a state of near nervous collapse, and although the ghostly Miss Terwilliger didn't fully understand what they were so upset about, she could see that they were genuinely distraught, so she did her best to help them as only she could. It completely backfired.

For Brittnee, Miss Terwilliger mixed a scent that would conjure memories of her childhood room and all the lovely clothes her parents had bought for her. Unfortunately for Brittnee, it did indeed recall her childhood room, but instead of echoing a time of love and plenty, in Brittnee's mind it only underlined the many ways that her childhood room was not Sweat Shop International—no bright halogen lights, no shiny chrome fitting rooms, no clerks in headsets walking around and being surly in that way that made you feel like you were important—just a dowdy, friendly, familiar room of suburban childhood with a closetful of clothes. Where was the glamour? The sparkle? Where was the pounding music?

Upon smelling the scent Miss Terwilliger had created for her, Brittnee suffered an immediate and total nervous breakdown, unable to see how she would ever be able to reclaim the feeling that Sweat Shop International had given her.

For Selena, bereft of her many accustomed social networks for three entire hours the day before, Miss Terwilliger created a scent redolent of the schoolyard at recess—the slap of the skipping rope, the shouts of a literal circle of friends, standing around voicing their approval, support and affection. Unfortunately, more important to Selena than actually being with her friends was her ability to write things on Facebook so that her friends could click that little thumbs-up button that meant "I like this," or being able to send text messages such as "OMG u r so gr8 ;)" so that her friends could respond in similar text-speak. This kind of communication made her feel far more connected and loved than actually being with and conversing with her friends, and upon smelling Miss Terwilliger's scent, which had nothing to do with social networks or text messages, all her mind was filled with was images of get-togethers in pubs, happy gatherings and one-on-one visits of sincere friendship. There were no "Like" buttons, nor did she see how typing very quickly with her thumbs could fit into this picture. Selena suffered a conniption and had to be carried out by the medics who'd just finished loading Brittnee into an ambulance.

Meanwhile, the cancellation of her favourite TV show had left Kylie feeling adrift and without purpose—what was she going to do now that it wasn't on anymore? For her, Miss Terwilliger created a scent that brought to mind running through ravines, flying kites and climbing trees—actually doing things. However, such a scent simply underlined for

Kylie the way that real life wasn't really like it was on the big flat screen TV that sat on the sterile white wall of the condo she lived in with her boyfriend; it filled her head with the novel and overwhelming idea of actually doing something instead of just watching people on TV doing something. This unwelcome intrusion of thought caused Kylie to have a rather alarming seizure, but luckily the medics were still there and they called yet another ambulance to cart her away.

As she watched her three colleagues being loaded into their respective ambulances, Miss Terwilliger had the most alarming realization of all—in her 4000 years as a perfume-mixing ghost, she had, until now, always been able to mix scents that could put people in touch with the positive, constructive parts of their psyches. But now, "civilization" had finally produced a generation of people so lacking in substance that they were no longer in touch with anything even resembling a foundation of feeling or purpose. With a flash of panic, Miss Terwilliger realized that just as Brittnee, Selena and Kylie felt they could no longer get their worlds back, so now did Miss Terwilliger feel the same way about her world. Whatever purpose in life (or, in this case, afterlife) she may once have had was now gone. And with that, she simply ceased to be—gone like a scent on the wind.

Seeing Ghosts

Patti, Raj and Brendan decided on a hike to put Patti's new digital camera through its paces. They would wander up into the mountains, where she could take pictures of the spectacular scenery and figure out how to use the camera's many features. The three of them were friends from the office where they all worked. Now, a couple of hours into the hike, Raj and Brendan chuckled behind Patti's back as she struggled to get the camera to focus and take a picture. Rightly or wrongly, Patti had a reputation at the office as someone constantly stymied by technology, be it a computer printer, a fax machine or a doorknob. Her two friends tried not to laugh out loud as she cursed and swore under her breath, first trying to get the camera to turn on, then trying to make it focus and finally trying to take a picture.

"What are you trying a picture of anyway?" Brendan asked as Patti hunched over a rotten tree stump.

"These three black moths or butterflies or whatever they are," she said through clenched teeth. "The way the three of them are sitting it looks like a face with eyes and a mouth."

"And what's the problem?" Raj wanted to know.

"The stupid camera keeps saying it's taken a picture, but then when I try to look at it on the little screen, there's nothing there," Patti said.

"If we want to get to the clearing by lunch time, we should get going," said Brendan, ever mindful of the time. Patti put the camera in its case and followed her two friends, trying to put her camera-related frustrations aside.

When they got to the little alpine clearing where they were going to eat their lunch, Brendan said, "Can I try the camera?"

"Sure, knock yourself out," said Patti as she unslung the backpack from her shoulders.

Brendan took the camera out of its case, turned it on and said, "Hey, Raj, give us a smile." Raj looked over and grinned. There was a little beep as Brendan took the picture.

"See, Patti, it works just fine," said Brendan, looking down at the little display screen on the back of the camera. Then with a sickening note of dread in his voice, "Oh my god."

"What is it?" Patti asked as she and Raj hurried over and peered at the camera's display screen.

"Oh my god," they said together. The picture showed Raj's head and shoulders—but not his face. It was the face of a soul screaming in anguish; the eyes were two smears of black and the mouth a darkened gash.

"What the hell?" said Raj.

Wordlessly, Brendan put the camera back in its case and the three of them started getting lunch ready. Patti had brought a salad; Brendan, Thai noodles; and Raj, sweetened yogurt for dessert.

"These Thai noodles are great," said Raj. "How did you get them to taste so peanutty without using peanuts?"

"Oh, crap," said Brendan.

"You *forgot* I'm allergic to peanuts?" said Raj.

"I am so, so sorry," said Brendan.

"No, no, no," said Raj, rummaging around in his backpack. He pulled out his epi-pen and jabbed it into his leg.

Still, as his horrified friends watched, over the next few minutes Raj's eyes swelled shut and his lips became hideously swollen. Brendan pulled Patti aside.

"He says he'll be okay," said Brendan. "We just need to wait for the swelling to go down, but does his face remind you of anything?"

"It reminds me of the creepy picture on the camera," said Patti.

"Me too," agreed Brendan, waving away some flying insects with an impatient gesture.

"You don't suppose that…" Patti didn't finish her sentence.

"The camera can see the future?" Brendan finished it for her. "No, not really." He swiped savagely at a persistent mosquito. Brendan enjoyed camping and was unfazed by all of nature's discomforts, except one—insects—which he put up with, but neither happily, graciously nor peacefully.

"Hey," called Raj from a few feet away, where he was reclining against a log, "this thing doesn't work for me either." They looked over to see him futilely inspecting the display screen. "I just tried to take a picture of Brendan, but no dice. By the way, this creepy picture from before, where I look like the devil—is this kind of what I look like now? Be honest."

"Well, kind of," said Brendan.

"You're supposed to lie," said Raj, who had been ragging on Brendan nonstop for forgetting about his peanut allergy.

"You look nothing like that," lied Patti, going over to Raj and taking the camera from him.

"Do you think the camera took a picture of me as I was *going* to appear?" joked Raj.

"No, not at all," said Patti rather unconvincingly. "Look, I'll try again." She took a few steps back and took a photo of Raj, and then gasped in horror.

"Now what?" said Raj, scrambling up and coming over to her. Brendan came over too, and they both gasped as they looked at the display screen. The camera had finally taken a picture for Patti—it showed Raj leaning against the log, his features still swollen, as indeed they were. But looming over

Raj was a ghostly image of Brendan with his face twisted into a demonic grimace, looking for all the world as though he was unleashing the very powers of hell upon Raj.

"You look like you're possessed," Patti told Brendan.

"Well now we know the camera's not telling the future," said Brendan. "I never get that angry." It was true—Brendan was famously even tempered and, except when insects were involved, rarely lost his temper.

The three friends whiled away the early afternoon with Raj good-naturedly ribbing Brendan as the swellings on his face gradually diminished. Finally Brendan and Raj decided to take short naps before they set out on the hike back down the mountain. Patti kept fiddling with the camera. She pointed it at her slumbering friends and pressed the button again. Nothing. She swore under her breath.

And now, we reach the truly tragic part of the story—the part where friendships collapse because of good intentions gone awry. Brendan had just wanted to make a nice lunch to share with his friends, but had sadly forgotten about Raj's peanut allergy. Raj was actually quite angry about this but tried to diffuse his anger through pointed barbs that were only half joking. Brendan felt awful about his friend's allergic reaction, which he fully recognized as being his fault, but because Raj didn't seem too upset, he was trying not to dwell on it. Patti, for her part, resented her friends' heavy-handed jokes about her inability to navigate any sort of technology and was beginning to feel that, perhaps, they were right. Still, if Brendan hadn't been just then having a dream about insects, all might have been well.

Flailing about in his sleep, swiping at the buzzing mosquitoes of his dreams, Brendan cuffed Raj on his still swollen, tender features. They both woke up immediately. An apology had formed itself on Brendan's lips, but Raj jokingly said, "Hey, watch out. You trying to kill me—again?"

And then Brendan, the one who rarely got mad, got mad—very mad. "Look, I'm sorry, sorry, *sorry* for damn well forgetting you have a peanut allergy! Would you just give it a rest?!"

"Looks like that camera *can* see the future," said Raj, looking up at Brendan standing above him. "I've never seen you this angry."

"It *cannot* see the future," said Patti. "Watch." Desperate to keep the peace between her friends, she turned the camera toward her own face, took a picture and then, without even looking, advanced toward them, holding out the camera's display screen. "See? Nothing, nothing at all."

But when she looked at their faces looking at the display screen, her heart sank. Patti turned the camera around to see that when she had taken the picture, she had blinked, looking for all the world as though she was dead. More disturbing were the ghostly images of Raj and Brendan, stretched on the ground behind her, also apparently dead.

"Dammit! Dammit!" said Patti.

"If that thing can see the future, then we're all going to die," said Raj.

"We are not going to die," said Brendan. "We have to stick together."

"Why?" snapped Patti. "So I can listen to both of you making fun of me behind my back?"

"So you can try to kill me again with your deadly noodles?" snapped Raj.

"Fine!" shouted Brendan. "Good bye and good luck." And with that, he grabbed his backpack and stormed off down the side of the mountain. Patti grabbed her stuff and left a few minutes later. Raj lay down again by the log and tried to calm down.

Unfortunately, Brendan, who was angrily rushing down the path, tripped and fell over a cliff, dying instantly on impact. Patti, unable to remember which end of the compass needle indicated north, got hopelessly lost and was never heard from again. Upon awakening from his nap, Raj started to clean up the clearing before departing, but tripped and landed face first in the open container of leftover Thai noodles. He suffered another allergic reaction, which, combined with his already weakened condition, proved fatal.

NoSnap Corporation Recalls Faulty Cameras

The NoSnap Corporation has recalled its KRAP 150 line of digital cameras. The NoSnap spokesman said that a manufacturer's defect may cause problems with the camera's display screen. Even though nothing appears on the screen, the camera has actually taken a picture. The camera may also overwrite previously undisplayed images onto photos subsequently taken by the user. This means that some pictures may feature ghostly images of objects that the camera has already taken photos of, resulting in a sort of digital double-exposure. The NoSnap Corporation has apologized for any inconvenience caused by the defect and is offering customers their money back.

Tag Along

I'm what you call a "graffiti artist." Hah! That's rich—I ain't no artist. I just like to bomb my tag all over town—sorry, I like to paint my name all over town—in case you been sitting under a rock for the last 30 years, we like to use spray paint—in cans—cans that we spray the paint out of—I can talk slower if you like.

What I'm gonna tell you is true, but you won't believe me cuz I'm the only one seen it. 'Bout a month ago, I got tired of all the heat I take for painting over other people's tags. It's gonna happen—a city this big and only so many walls, you're gonna get people tagging over you. I don't care. I live with it. I can always go back and tag again. But some people—they say if you paint over their tag then you're disrespecting them and they get mad and they find you, they probably pop a cap in your ass. Sorry? Oh, that's how we say "They'll probably shoot you" in plain English. Was it comfy under that rock?

I don't want no cap in my ass, but I also don't want to stop tagging, so my answer is to use glow-in-the-dark paint. It's clear in the light—invisible—but if you get into a nice dark alley you can see my sig right there, glowing like one of those bracelets little girls take to boy band concerts but all twisted up in a sick-looking knot. When I started, my tag looked sort of like the letters of my name, but now it's just a shape that means…me. I'm the only one who knows it means me, and I like to keep it that way.

Since I started using the glow-in-the-dark paint, my favourite alley is this one over the west end of town. It's got a security light but no security camera, and it's way out of anyone's way. The security light has a motion detector that makes it come on when you walk into the alley, but it goes off again after two minutes and everything is real dark. So what I do is I go in and spray my tag and the light stays on as long as I'm moving around. Then when I'm done, I go stand in the shadows and wait for the light to go out and when it does, I can see my tag, right there, glowing in the dark. I like that time when I'm standing there waiting for the light to go off—gives me time to think.

So this one night, I'm there in my favourite alley and I've just finished my tag and I go over to stand in the shadows and after a couple minutes the light goes out. Then I pretty much crap myself cuz I can see my tag, but I also see that someone else has started using glow-in-the-dark paint and I've painted over his tag and it's X-Ray.

X-Ray's real name is Ray something or other, but he's a real gangsta—word is he once blew some guy away for painting over his tag—that and the other guy had a tag that also started with X and X-Ray didn't like that. I've never met him but I've heard all about him. Not a homey whose tag you wanna be painting over.

I'm standing there too scared to move when I see that down by the corner at the far end of the alley, somebody else has been busy with glowing paint and they've painted the shape of a person, life-sized, just standing there with its arms at its sides.

Then I see it move. It waves at me. Friendly sort of, but I'm not expecting it and I jump and trigger the motion detector light. It comes on and all it shows me is the empty alley, with the wall all covered in swirls and letters and neon paints of other people's tags—but no glowing shape of a person. Now I'm what you call curious, so I take a good look around but all that's there is nothing. I figure I'll never find out anything with the light on, so I go across the street and wait at the corner.

Finally the motion-detector light goes out again, and I stand there, feeling like a fool. All I can see is X-Ray's tag glowing in the dark and mine too, painted over it. Then at the far end of the wall I see it again. It slips around the corner like a glowing shadow and creeps along the wall like it's on tiptoe, doesn't want anyone to see it. When it gets to the corner of the alley it goes around the corner too, like a glowing shadow.

The hairs on my neck are standing up. I watch it go along the wall of the alley like it's projected there or something. And now I can see its head turning back and forth—I think it's looking for me. Well, I ain't looking *for* it, but I can't stop looking *at* it. I know I'm hidden and it can't see me. It stands there for a minute and then, I swear, it scratched its head like it was trying to figure out what to do. Finally, it was like it could spray ghost paint or something, because it puts its arm up and starts to paint a tag:

I M XLNT

"I am excellent," since you was probably wondering, what with being under that rock for so long. I know this tag. Used to be you'd see it around all over the city, but then it slowly got painted over and didn't come back. But now here it was getting bombed by some glowing light thing in my favourite alleyway. Come to think of it, this alley was XLNT's favourite for a while too and I remember seeing his tag here. Guess he'd never gone away.

Now I decide to be courageous and walk over there. XLNT sees me coming and runs up to the corner and waves at me. Then I trip the motion detector and it all vanishes when the alley lights up. But I'm patient and sit there against the wall like I usually do and wait. When the light goes out again, it's standing there, sort of leaning against the edge of a doorway with its arms folded. It stands up and gets to work with its phantom spray can and writes:

X-RAY NOT B PLEASED. I CAN HELP U. NEED U 2 HELP ME.

"Okay," I said out loud. I could do that without setting off the motion-detector light.

XLNT got busy again with his spray bomb:

GO 2 MAILBOX IN PARK. BOMB MY TAG— XLNT—ON FRNT OF BOX. USE GLOW PAINT. COME BACK TMRRW NIGHT.

"Okay," I said again, and I left. I did just like XLNT bombed me to. I went over to the park, found the mailbox and bombed "XLNT" across the front in big invisible letters. There was a security light here, too, that flicked on the second I got there, but I didn't care. When I was done I walked back into the shadows and waited. When the light flicked off I could see that I'd spray painted XLNT's tag right over top of another tag—X-Ray. I went home and slept better than I had for ages.

The next night I thought I had a pretty good idea of what was going to happen—I was way, way wrong. Well actually, I was partly right. Anyway, I stood across the street in the shadows and waited. After a while I heard footsteps and see this big huge fat guy walking down the street all covered in bling, everything in the shape of an X. I'm guessing this is X-Ray and the way he's walking, I can tell he's P.O.'d.

I know these types. Every night they tour around and check their tags to see if anyone has bombed over them. I'm willing to bet he's just come from the mailbox in the park. I watch him come down the street. He stops at the alley and the security light clicks on. He knows what he's looking for though and stands there, like a beached whale but with legs and bling. Finally the light flicks off and you hear him say "Dammit!" and the lights come and he's just thrown his hat on the ground. He stands there huffing and puffing like hippo—or maybe a buffalo—I don't know.

Then, without any warning, way sooner than two minutes, the security light goes out and you can see XLNT's glowing shape on the wall. X-Ray swore and the light snapped on in time for me to see him whip this huge gat out of his pocket and start shooting at the wall where XLNT had been. Then the lights went out again and stayed out. X-Ray shot some more at the glowing shape, but in a second his ammo ran out and it was just the clicking of the hammer. Then the glowing ghost of XLNT pretty clearly gave him the finger and X-Ray just got madder and madder and finally pulled out a can of spray paint and started blindly spraying at the wall, trying to cover the whole surface like it could get rid of XLNT—but it couldn't.

And then, I still don't know how he did it, but the glowing ghost of XLNT sort of waved his arms or cast a spell or something and all of a sudden, X-Ray got this terrified look on his face and started sort of choking and it looked like he was trying to pry his fingers off the button of the spray bomb but couldn't. He just kept spraying and choking until his eyes rolled back into his head and he fell on his knees, his one finger still holding down the spray button until there was no more paint, just the hiss of the gas from the can. X-Ray's body fell over dead and the spray can clattered to the ground. And then this sort of glowing stuff started coming out of his mouth and going onto the wall like paint, and at the same time XLNT's shape started to peel off the wall and streamed into the nozzle of the spray can. So now XLNT was in the spray can, and X-Ray's big fat glowing shape was there on the wall—just like XLNT's had been before. He looked around and then started pounding his fists on the brick like he was trying to get out. He was probably screaming too, but like I could hear him.

I knew what I had to do. I walked over and set off the motion detector and the light snapped on. X-Ray's graffiti ghost disappeared but his body was still lying on the ground. I walked around it, real careful, and picked up the spray can. Then I walked over to the park and found a nice dark spot, far away from the lights. I pressed down the button on the spray bomb and this sort of glowing gas started to come out and form itself into a shape in front of me. I held the button down until there was nothing left, and then I watched as XLNT rose up into the sky and went off into the galaxy, probably to tag it with light.

After about a month of asking around I finally found out the name of the bomber X-Ray had iced for painting over his tag in glowing paint. The kid's name was Alexander or Xander—or it could of been Xavier or something like that—but I didn't care. I knew it was XLNT, and that was good enough for me.

Ghost in the Machine

Heloise Fallow, Ms. Fallow to her students, was probably the most unpopular teacher in the school. She was utterly humourless and permitted no hint of warmth to soften her frosty demeanour. She taught science. All day long, she tried to mould the minds of her teenage charges into efficient engines of reason and logic. Ms. Fallow's goal was probably unrealistic; she taught grades 10 and 11, comprising a particularly rowdy bunch of teens whose brains, far from being efficient engines of reason and logic, seemed, in fact, to be unbalanced contraptions of wildly firing hormones, fanciful notions and delusional convictions. Really they were just a bunch of regular kids, trying to define the world for themselves, pushing, testing and trying—Ms. Fallow certainly found them to be trying, at any rate.

Her one island of calm in this storm of hijinks, high fives and high spirits was Cornelius, a rather skinny, pimply boy with a brain as ordered and mercilessly logical as her own. He scored in the high nineties on all tests and assignments, and whenever she turned around from the blackboard to quell the noisy chaos in the classroom, Cornelius was sitting there calmly, either taking notes or regarding her owlishly through his thick glasses. Occasionally they would even exchange pleasantries after class. For instance, they were both keen to witness the upcoming Zenith meteor shower, which only appeared every 150 years. Or, another time, they briefly discussed the merits of faith versus science and, hardly surprisingly, agreed that science was the hands-down winner.

The other teachers at the school found Heloise to be as much of a cold fish as did her students. At lunch in the staff room, she kept to herself, either marking tests, grading essays or, in moments of rare leisure, leafing through the latest science magazine. Her Saturdays and Sundays were spent much the same way and, come Monday, there were never any weekend adventures to relate to her colleagues. But, unbeknownst to Ms. Fallow's colleagues and students, beneath it all was a great heart, longing for companionship, wanting, though not daring, to believe that she might still find her match, a man whose mind was, if not congruent to her own, at least complementary.

On the first night of the Zenith meteor shower, Heloise prudently took a nap when she got home from school—after all, it was going to be a late night. Then she went out into her backyard and peered through her telescope. The darting, flashing steaks of light were beautiful. They made her think—just as the meteors shot across the sky and were gone, life too was just a brief light in the surrounding darkness. If she wanted to meet someone, she had better do something about it.

After admiring the meteor shower a bit longer, she went back into the house and sat down at her computer. About a month ago she had joined SciDate. It was a dating website for science-types, but after joining, she hadn't ever actually looked at it again. Now she logged in and noticed that there was a special live chat room called Zenith Meteor Admirers. Pleased, she clicked on it and saw that there was only one other user there—someone whose username was Abelard. Well that appealed to her immediately; Abelard and Heloise had been two star-crossed lovers in the 12th century, drawn to one another by their love of learning and philosophy.

Abelard had typed a series of dots and dashes. It was Morse code. Heloise was surprised but pleased. Here was someone who enjoyed using the old terms from the

days of HAM radio and telegraphs. Heloise, of course, knew
Morse code and instantly divined that Abelard had typed
"C-Q," meaning "Calling any stations." Or, in effect, "Is any-
one there?"

She clicked on the reply bar and typed "Hello."

There was a short pause and then Abelard typed another
message in Morse code: "G-E" for "Good evening."

Heloise also typed "G-E."

The rest of their conversation went as follows.

ABELARD: *Are you enjoying the meteor shower
tonight?*

HELOISE: *I am. Are you?*

ABELARD: *Yes. Beautiful.*

HELOISE: *Abelard your real name?*

ABELARD: *Yes. Heloise yours?*

HELOISE: *Yes.*

ABELARD: *We are like those well-read lovers of long
ago. H-E-E.*

Here, Heloise realized that Abelard had used old telegrapher lingo—H-E-E for "Humour intended." She typed back
"L-O-L."

ABELARD: *What is L-O-L?*

Heloise thought that was certainly strange. Everyone these
days knew that L-O-L stood for "laughing out loud" if one was
emailing or text messaging with someone else. Why, she'd
even recently heard one of her students say "L-O-L" instead of
actually laughing. She now found herself wishing that

Abelard, whoever he might be, was joking, but she typed back simply, "Short for Laughing Out Loud."

ABELARD: *I see. Glad you like my joke. Feel lucky to see meteors. Next time they appear will be 2011.*

HELOISE: *What do you mean?*

ABELARD: *Zenith meteors only appear every 150 years. Next time will be 2011.*

HELOISE: *It is 2011.*

ABELARD: *You are funny.*

Heloise sat back and frowned at the computer for a minute. Then she typed, "What year is it where you are? H-E-E."

ABELARD: *1861. Same as where you are.*

Heloise perceived an odd sensation as though an icy finger were tracing the length of her spine. For the first time in her life, the hairs on the back of her neck stood up. But then she was angry. Abelard was teasing her and she did not appreciate it. Why, this was just silly—as if a tunnel in time could exist between someone operating a telegraph and someone on a modern computer. Why would an educated man, who presumably wanted to date an educated woman, resort to such an irritating device? She angrily slammed the lid of her laptop closed and went to bed.

But Heloise couldn't sleep. Although she didn't actually believe someone was communicating with her through time, a part of her desperately *wanted* to believe it. She even got up for a few minutes and pulled out an old magazine with an article about quantum viewing, the idea that, although time travel itself was impossible, we might be able to *see* other periods of time. It was, at least, a theoretical possibility.

Then she tried to sleep again, but still couldn't, so she put on her housecoat and went outside to look at the meteors. They would only be visible for two more nights. She bent down to the eyepiece to admire the glowing shower of light once more—then stood up straight. *The meteors.* Was it possible, however unlikely, that the meteors could somehow create a temporal connection between an analogue telegrapher in 1861 and a digital lonely heart in 2011? No it was *not* possible; in fact it was ridiculous, and she returned to her sleepless bed.

The next afternoon after classes Heloise exchanged some hurried pleasantries with Cornelius, then hurried home and tried to nap but couldn't. She paced around asking herself the same question over and over again. Why? Why would a man who had joined SciDate introduce something so ridiculously whimsical as time travel? Then she shook her head—who cared if he was being whimsical? Perhaps it was because he wanted to get to know her better. She had read an article somewhere about playfulness as a tool in attracting a mate; perhaps Abelard had read the same article. Tonight, she vowed, she would approach their chat (if there was one) in the same spirit of quaint jocularity.

After observing the meteors for about an hour, Heloise once more signed on to SciDate, went to the Zenith Meteor Admirers link, and there he was, still the only one in the chat room. She sat for a minute, composed her thoughts and then started typing.

HELOISE: *Greetings from 2011.*

ABELARD: *Heloise. You didn't say goodbye last night.*

HELOISE: *Sorry. Had to go.*

ABELARD: *You are the fastest sender I have ever seen.*

As she had the night before, Heloise noticed that Abelard was not a fast typist—just a couple of characters every second or two. Now, his comment that she was a fast sender made a strange kind of sense; someone transmitting via Morse code (or who was pretending to transmit via Morse code) would only be able to tap out a single "letter" at the rate of perhaps one per second, much slower than typing with a keyboard. Heloise had to admire Abelard's commitment to his ruse, or whatever it was. The conversation continued.

HELOISE: *Tell me about yourself. Who is your favourite author?*

ABELARD: *Mr. Dickens.*

Heloise sat up a little straighter; *her* favourite author was Charles Dickens. She decided to lay a little trap for Abelard and typed, "My favourite book of his is *Great Expectations*. Yours?"

ABELARD: *You must live in England. G.E. just finished its run there but is not yet published here in former colonies. H-E-E.*

Well Abelard had proven his worth once more—it was true that *Great Expectations* had finished its first serialization in Britain in 1861 but was not published in North America until later that same year. No matter what time he claimed to exist in, Abelard might be just the man she had been looking for. Heloise typed, "I don't live in England. Canada. You?"

ABELARD: *USA.*

HELOISE: *Some trouble there I think.*

Heloise was testing him again—true, he was probably just sitting at his computer looking up the answers to her questions as he typed them, character by painful character, but it was still kind of fun.

Abelard sent a reply: "Yes. The southern states are trying to secede. My heart is sad for my country."

He'd gotten that one right too—the southern states had tried to secede early in 1861, sparking the American Civil War. He was good; she had to give him that. She noticed he was typing some more.

ABELARD: *So much turmoil here. So much fear. Glad to find a friend.*

HELOISE: *I'm glad to find a friend too. Also seek companionship.*

ABELARD: *Me too. But travel is perilous during this civil war.*

HELOISE: *Can we stop pretending it's 1861 please?*

ABELARD: *What do you mean?*

HELOISE: *Let's talk like it's 2011, because it is.*

Now there was a long pause. Heloise typed, "Are you still there?"

ABELARD: *Yes. Sorry but it is 1861.*

As she read what he wrote, Heloise felt another chill go down her spine. Was this really happening? Was she really communicating with a man 150 years in the past? Was she really having feelings for a man 150 years in the past? More importantly, was she in fact really having feelings for a man, period? She typed back, "I cannot believe this. I am a woman of science."

ABELARD: *I am man of science but I do believe it. The telegraph would have seemed like magic 100 years ago but it is science. Perhaps the meteors are doing it.*

HELOISE: *Sorry, but I cannot accept that this is happening. You are alive in my time and that is that.*

ABELARD: *So in 2011 science has eradicated belief?*

HELOISE: *Yes. As it ought.*

ABELARD: *Then I am sorry for you. In 1861 science and wonder go hand in hand as they ought. As we ought. If only you could believe.*

She pushed back her chair. He wasn't just challenging her to believe that communication through time was possible. He was challenging her to believe that a man could love her—and that she could love him back. She took a deep breath and typed, "If we really are 150 years apart then holding hands is not an option. If this is all real and the meteors are the cause of this then you will know that after the meteor shower passes tomorrow night we will not be able to communicate again. Let us sign-off for now, but decide what our final words shall be tomorrow night."

Heloise thought that this ultimatum would surely shake Abelard out of his strange game of make-believe. Or if, against all odds, they were somehow communicating through time, maybe some kind of corroborating evidence might come out of their final communication together.

Abelard typed, "Very well. G-E."

The next day, Heloise brushed off Cornelius when he tried to ask her about last night's meteor shower and rushed home. She fretted about the house, not even attempting to nap, barely glanced at the meteors when they started and finally, at about 10 o'clock, settled down to the chat session.

Abelard was again the only one in the Zenith Meteor Admirers chat room. As soon as she logged on, he began, one painfully slow letter at a time: "Heloise, in my time, love is something that requires belief, not proof. But if you will not put your faith in me, then at least perhaps I can prove to you that I am real. If you will tell me where you live, I will arrange for a photo and letter from me to be mailed to you 150 years from now."

And with that, Heloise knew the game was over. Poetic as his words may have been, anyone living in the 1860s would not have said "photo," but rather "tintype," "daguerre-otype" or even "photograph." That and the fact that his final communication to her had requested information about her location. Without replying, she turned off the computer and went outside to look at the meteors for the last time.

The next day, Heloise went to the police with her strange tale of the online lurker from 150 years in the past. To her surprise, they took it rather seriously and promised to make inquiries. With the co-operation of SciDate, it took the police less than a month to discover that Abelard was, of course, Cornelius. She realized that she had somehow known that all along.

"Why did you do it?" she asked him over the table at the police station.

"It was a test," he said simply. "I wondered if, under enough pressure, you might err on the side of belief instead of science. You didn't. Well done."

Cornelius wasn't charged with any crime, but he was taken out of Ms. Fallow's class and sent to a different school. They never saw each other again.

For the rest of her lonely days, Heloise was haunted—not by ghosts or spirits, but by ideas, two ideas in particular. First, that were it not for a 30-year difference in their ages, she and Cornelius might have really gotten on, or, when she was in a more playful frame of mind, that were it not for the 150 years separating them, she and Abelard might have really had something. Second, and more disturbingly, she couldn't help but feel that, had she been able to believe that somewhere in the past her ideal lover had lived, even though she would have been wrong, she might have been happy.

Iron Eyes Weeps

Police baffled by flayed bodies

Police reported the discovery of two bodies (both males) under an east-end bridge this morning. Both bodies appeared to have had the skin stripped off. Police are not saying how they think the men died, but the deaths are being treated as suspicious.

Chad and Thirsk were a couple of extreme dudes—at least in their own minds. Really, they did most of the things they did because they saw the circle of people around them doing the same or similar things. They were both very fit, a result of pumping iron until they felt "the rage" and then chugging protein drinks. They both drove gas-guzzling vehicles that had terrible mileage. They both lived in condos with brittle beauties, whose microscopic dogs they could be observed angrily walking on most mornings before work. They both drenched themselves in body spray, which they assumed made them chick magnets, when in fact it gave anyone in a 15-foot radius a splitting headache. But they actually were different from most of us in three ways: first, it had never *occurred* to them that they could do things differently than they did; second, neither one was *willing* to do things differently; and third, they didn't *care* about the effects of their choices.

On weekends they ditched their girlfriends (who were secretly relieved), roared out to the mountains in their unnecessarily large vehicles (taking both when one would do), and set up camp at the base of a cliff to do some rock climbing. All weekend they blared music, littered the area with their unfiltered cigarette butts and knocked back can after can of an energy drink whose main ingredients were caffeine and sugar. Then they scattered the cans to and fro amid the packaging from their scientifically formulated Muscle Meals, instant food that contained no natural ingredients and came in a foil pouch, surrounded by a plastic envelope, protected by a layer of extra-pliable five-colour cardboard that was made from old-growth rainforest.

One night, when an excess of caffeine had caused their eyes to start twitching back and forth in their sockets, a ghost appeared to them. In contrast to Chad and Thirsk's manic state of twitching irritability, the ghost was still and calm. He was clad simply in the garb of a tribal chief and regarded them sadly through steady, dark eyes.

"I am Iron Eyes," the ghost said. "I lived here during life and in death I am the guardian of this place. I speak for the spirits in the trees, the stones and the water. I speak for the animals who make their homes here. I speak for those who cannot speak."

"Holy crap!" said Chad.

"Whoa!" said Thirsk.

"I am here to warn you," said the ghost of Iron Eyes. "You must stop your thoughtless destruction of good things in this world. Your giant trucks destroy the air and the water, and the very process of making them destroys the earth. The unnecessary packaging from your synthetic meals is turning this place into a wasteland, as are the cans from your noxious drinks. Your obsession with fitness is not a quest for health, but rather the pursuit of vanity. You do not smoke

tobacco to celebrate peace, but rather to fulfill unclean crav-
ings, leaving your burnt and charred detritus here to con-
taminate the soil. The foul-smelling mist you spray on
yourselves poisons the air and destroys the atmosphere.
Stop these things if you would avoid my wrath."

"Wrath this!" said Thirsk, and he sprayed some body
spray at Iron Eyes. It simply passed through the ghost.

"And here, have some of my obnoxious drink," said
Chad, lobbing a half-full can of it at Iron Eyes. It also passed
through the ghost.

Iron Eyes shook his head sadly and faded away.

"He can't tell us what to do," said Chad.

"Well," said Thirsk, "I mean he can tell us, but we don't
have to listen to him."

And with that, they hopped into their trucks and went
back to town.

As soon as they each got home, their girlfriends' microscopic dogs growled at them suspiciously and their girlfriends themselves complained about the odd smell that
seemed to accompany them—like stale cigarette butts. Chad
attempted to blame the smell on his girlfriend's having left
water in the vegetable steamer, but she only ate processed
frozen vegetables, microwaved until all the nutrients had
been irradiated out of them, so this was unlikely. Thirsk
tried to blame the smell on the only truly living thing in the
apartment—a small cactus on the window sill. What he
didn't realize was that his girlfriend kept the cactus around
because it reminded her of herself, and so this ploy didn't
exactly go over well either.

The smell of stale cigarette butts seemed to waft out of
their pores and only got stronger as the week went on. Chad
and Thirsk doused themselves in body spray, but it didn't do

any good. Within the month, both girlfriends had kicked them out because of the overwhelming odour of ash and grime that seemed to follow them everywhere. And within a week after that, they'd both been fired from their jobs for "olfactory infractions" (a fancy way of saying they smelled bad, though they were too dumb to understand this).

Reduced to living in their trucks, a new problem arose when they tried to dump a month's worth of accumulated Muscle Meal packaging into the river—the next morning it mysteriously appeared back in their trucks, sodden, rotten and smelly, as though it had just come back from a dip in a particularly polluted part of the river. No matter how often they tried to dump it, it just came right back and they soon found themselves being cramped in by a steadily encroaching wall of foil pouches, plastic envelopes and extra-pliable five-colour cardboard made from old-growth rainforest. Each one secretly suspected the other of sneaking out in the night, fishing the garbage out of the river and returning it to the vehicles. Such was their vacuous mental state that it did not occur to them to ask *why* the other would do this, but the notion festered illogically in each of their enfeebled minds.

Since the packaging was building up, one day, amazingly, it occurred to them to try eating foods that did not come in packages. Lacking even the most rudimentary of cooking skills they simply bought a bunch of carrots and dug in— and spat them out in a hurry when the insides of their mouths started to burn as though they had ingested acid. And so it was with any natural food they tried to eat; broccoli, potatoes, cauliflower, lettuce, apples, oranges and bananas all burned the insides of their mouths, leaving blisters and bits of flayed skin hanging off. Even water produced a nasty burning sensation, and they brought it up shortly after drinking it anyway.

Soon, reduced to a steady diet of Muscle Meals and energy drinks, they noticed that their bodies were becoming hyper-defined and that they were fast approaching the point of having zero body fat. Initially they were puzzled by this since they hadn't worked out in weeks, their gyms having cancelled their memberships shortly after they lost their jobs. Eventually though, they simply accepted their status as awesome dudes with effortlessly buff bodies.

Unable to drink water or eat natural foods, their minds became more and more addled, and the curious definition of their bodies continued to grow sharper until their muscles began to break through their skin, which eventually fell off altogether. Soon each one looked like a flayed anatomical exhibit, all the skin having been stripped off to reveal muscle, bone and tendon. Whenever either of them sat down on the leather seats of their vehicles, their limbs made a sound like a steak landing on a cutting board. The overall impression brought to mind a full-colour scientific diagram out of *Gray's Anatomy*, crossed with poster art from a low-budget zombie film.

"Holy crap, Chad!" said Thirsk, his eyes rolling creepily in their sockets. "You look like you're in one of those Cadaver Universe exhibits where they take all the skin off of dead bodies and then pose them playing poker and dancing and stuff."

"So do you!" said Chad, his skeletal grin looking more foolish than ever. "But you look like the dead guy they posed on the toilet!"

"Well you look like the dead guy they posed walking his dead girlfriend's little tiny dead dog," Thirsk countered.

And with that, they attacked each other, the wet slap of their exposed muscles echoing through the night as they attempted to punch, grapple, choke and generally slaughter one another. Iron Eyes appeared and watched them sadly— he was glad that Chad and Thirsk would shortly no longer be able to poison the earth, water and air, but he wished they had never poisoned them to begin with. Presently, the noises stopped and the two odd-looking bodies grew still, each having managed to strangle the other.

The ghost of Iron Eyes faded away.

3
A Ghostly Miscellany

The Fortress of Solitude

Robert Misan was one of those lonely souls whose friends
were really acquaintances. Nonetheless, he kept photos of
them lined up on a little table under the window in his tiny
bachelor apartment. It was embarrassing, but he kept them
there to make himself feel as though he had true friends. In
reality, he worked hard to make sure that no one but himself
ever crossed the threshold of his doorway.

Truth be known, as well as being painfully shy, Robert
was utterly paranoid—he worried constantly about burglars
breaking into his apartment and, indeed, this fear seemed to
have extended itself into his social life, with a fear of anyone
coming to visit, or for that matter, getting too close in any
sense. He combatted this fear by installing a battery of locks
and other safeguards to prevent break-ins, or at least alert
him as to whether someone had tried to gain entrance to his
apartment while he was out.

Every time he left his apartment, he scattered a light
dusting of flour on his floor, even though it made a mess, so
he would see if anyone had walked across his floor while he
was out. Then once he had closed the door and was out in
the hall, he turned four different keys in four different locks
and finished by snapping a padlock closed at the bottom of
the door. Finally, he pulled a hair from his head and, using
his spit as glue, pressed the hair across the gap between
the door and the door frame—if it wasn't there when he
returned, then he would know that someone had opened the
door while he was away.

Tonight, he was heading out to the bar to meet one of his
acquaintances, Brian, for a drink. Brian was the I.T. special-
ist at Robert's office and was constantly baffled as to why

Robert never wanted to go out in a group, but always insisted that social interactions be one-on-one. Robert, frankly, was baffled as to why he felt this way too, but he did. Brian's photo (taken in the office during a moment of shared triumph after they had figured out why Robert's e-mail account sent out multiple copies of the same message) was the first in the row of photos that Robert kept under his window.

Their drinks tonight were as they always were; Brian tried to draw Robert out of his shell, and Robert just receded further inward. Robert returned to his apartment no different than when he left. He inspected the hair across the gap between the door and the door frame—it was intact and he carefully removed it. Next, he undid the padlock at the bottom of the door and then twisted the four different keys in the four different locks. He entered the apartment and turned on the light in one fluid move, his heart pounding as he saw that…the flour was undisturbed.

Robert heaved a sigh of relief and walked into the room, grabbed the dust-buster he kept by the door and vacuumed up the flour. Then he flopped down on the couch and turned on the TV. As he always did after one of his outings, he turned to look at the little row of photos. *Brian's photo was lying face down on the table.*

Robert felt as though his heart had stopped beating. How could someone have gotten into his apartment? The hair was in place, the locks were locked and there had been no footprints in the flour. He reasoned that it must have been a freak air current, a minor earthquake or even the vibrations from a large truck driving past.

Then the phone rang and his heart nearly exploded.

"Hello?"

"Robert, it's Julia from work." Julia sat in the cubicle across from him. Hers was the second photo in his strange little gallery beneath the window. It sounded as though she was crying.

"Julia, what's wrong?"

"I just got a call from Rick." Rick was their supervisor at work and the third photo on Robert's table. "It's Brian," sobbed Julia. "He was killed by a truck crossing the street."

"But I was just with him at the bar!" said Robert.

"Well," Julia wept, "he's gone now. Listen, I have to phone some other people but I wanted to let you know. Goodbye." She hung up.

Robert sat there looking at Brian's down-turned photo. It was a staggering coincidence. Had Brian possibly been killed by the same truck that had caused the vibrations that knocked the photo over?

After a restless sleep, Robert took extra precautions the next day as he left for work. He sprinkled a light dusting of flour on the frames of the photos themselves and then walked backward out of the apartment, spreading a fine coating on the floor starting at the feet of the little table and trailing all the way to the door, with plenty of coverage in between. Then he picked up his tools, which he'd left by the door, and went out into the hallway, where he installed a hasp for a second padlock at the top of the door. Placing his tools back in the apartment, just inside the door, he then snapped the new padlock closed at the top of the door, twirled all four keys in all four locks, snapped the bottom padlock closed and then carefully spit-pasted no less than three hairs across the gap between the door and the frame. Satisfied at last, but still nervous, he headed to work.

The mood at the office was sombre. Brian had been well known and well liked. Everyone moped around, glassy eyed and sad. After work, Robert, Rick, Julia and a few others went to an informal gathering at the bar, where they glumly and tearfully reminisced. Robert was surprised to find that, even though it was a sad occasion, he didn't really mind being out with a group of people—it wasn't so bad after all. Paradoxically, he went home feeling better and less generally strange than he had for years.

He stood in front of his door and inspected his safeguards. All three hairs were in place and all four locks, plus the two padlocks, seemed fine. Inside, as he did every night, Robert flicked the lights on quickly, steeling himself for an unwanted intruder. The empty room stared back at him. Carefully examining the flour on the floor, he was glad to see a complete lack of any marks or footsteps. But then he looked up at his little photo table and froze in his tracks— the second and third photos, Julia's and Rick's, were gone. Looking around the room frantically he saw them, lying neatly, side by each, on the couch—fully six feet from the table where they had started the day, both face down.

In a panicked sweat Robert tip-toed forward, looking desperately for any trace of an intruder, but all of the flour was intact—even that which he'd sprinkled on the frames of the photos. Robert's worst nightmare had come true: some-one—or as he was now forced to concede, some*thing*—had been in his apartment and moved the photos without leaving any sort of a trace. He found himself wishing for the first time that he wasn't alone.

The next day Robert walked into the office and was stunned to learn that both Rick and Julia had been killed the night before. Julia had somehow fallen into the river, and Rick had perished when he jumped in to try to save her.

Immediately Robert thought of their photos neatly laid face down on the couch. First Brian, now Rick and Julia—it couldn't be a coincidence. Robert tried to remember who was in the fourth and now sole photo on his table, and then with a jolt remembered that it was himself! The photo had been taken when Robert had exceeded his monthly quota and been named Employee of the Month.

Although he was a diligent employee (even in the face of tragedy), Robert now abandoned any pretense of work and set about surfing the web from his work station, trying to learn more about the force (or forces) that seemed to be at work in his life. He read about ghosts, doppelgangers, were-wolves and vampires before he got to poltergeists—perhaps he was being persecuted by a poltergeist. He was pursuing this line of research when he found himself on the web-page of the National Paranormal Society. The website was divided into local chapters, and he clicked on the name of his city, hoping that perhaps someone nearby could help him. And then, almost by accident, he clicked on the link for "Haunted Buildings in Your Area" and there it was—*the address of his apartment building and the number of his very unit!*

Robert read on, scarcely able to stop himself. His apartment was one of the city's most famously haunted landmarks! He briefly wondered why he didn't know this, but then considered that it wasn't the sort of thing you found out unless you were looking for it. Reading on, he discovered that his unit had been known for years to be haunted by a particularly anti-social poltergeist that, like Robert himself, did not appreciate its privacy being interrupted.

Well, this did at least explain why Robert's rent was so cheap, but why would the disturbances start now? He'd lived there for five years without any problems. And why would the poltergeist target Robert's coworkers, who had never even been to the apartment? Was it all a ploy to make Robert leave or kill him trying? Perhaps, thought Robert to himself, he wouldn't live there much longer anyway—he was starting to feel that perhaps he could be a little more sociable (the recent tragedies notwithstanding), and a haunted apartment was clearly not the place to entertain new friends.

Robert hatched a plan: he would go home cautiously, speak aloud his intention to leave, gather a few possessions and then simply go. Surely that would appease the poltergeist, and then the killing would stop. After all, the troubled spirit merely wanted its privacy, as, until recently, had Robert. He made his way home looking over his shoulder and peering overhead every couple of seconds, checking for unlikely means of death: falling pianos, rabid dogs, truckfuls of porcupines and so forth.

When he got to his door he didn't even bother checking the hairs, just opened all the locks and charged in. He had expected his own photograph to be turned face down, so he was surprised to see it standing up in its accustomed place on the little table beneath the window. He warily made his way into the room and noted that, as usual, the flour was undisturbed.

Robert gathered some clothes and his laptop, then stood in the centre of the room and proclaimed, "Poltergeist! I know you crave your privacy, so I shall give it to you. Today I am leaving this apartment, never to return."

Suddenly the room was filled with a violent wind that blasted the flour into a blizzard and then subsided as quickly

as it had come. As the fine dust settled, Robert saw that letters had been formed in the flour on the floor:

NO
LIKE YOU
ONLY YOU
DON'T LIKE OTHERS
YOU FRIEND
OTHERS WOULD HAVE COME HERE

And now, too late, Robert saw things for what they were.
The poltergeist, like himself, had decided it was ready for
some company, but just one-on-one company—no groups.
As anti-social as Robert had been, the poltergeist had sensed
his recent change of heart and started eliminating anyone
who might conceivably have interrupted their togetherness.

"Well," Robert said to the empty room, "I still choose to
leave. You can't make me stay. I've decided I'm ready to let
people in. Goodbye."

But as he turned to go, the door slammed shut and he
heard the bolts of the four locks snapping shut and then the
metallic click of the two padlocks closing on the other side
of the door. Robert stood there, looking at the door, feeling
all alone, but knowing he wasn't.

From the Cradle to the Grave

Like any parents, June and Howard loved their little girls. Deanna and Michelle had been born two years apart. Fascinated by her new little sister, Deanna had dubbed Michelle "Meow" as she tried to sputter the baby's name from her two-year-old lips. And as "Meow" herself reached the age of baby babble, she had responded in kind, calling her big sister "Deedo." The two sisters continued to call each other by these nicknames even when they were well past the prattling age. Somewhere along the way, they shortened the nicknames to "Me" and "Dee."

But it all came crashing to a horrible end when Deanna was eight and Michelle was six. One day, June and Howard woke up in the hospital. The last thing they could remember was getting into the car with the girls to go for supper at the family's favourite restaurant. The doctors told them that they were lucky to have survived being struck by the bus— Deanna and Michelle had not been so lucky.

June and Howard were broken in both body and spirit following the accident. As so often happens in cases like this, their broken bones healed long before their shattered souls. Aside from their grief for the girls' loss and the accompanying feelings of responsibility for their deaths, June and Howard also resented the fact that they couldn't remember anything after they got in the car to go to the restaurant. To judge from the time the accident had occurred and the direction they'd been going, they must have gotten to the restaurant and had supper—depositions from the wait-staff there confirmed this. But neither June nor Howard could remember any of it.

Other things were missing from their memories too, layers of their lives from before the accident. Their core group of friends were as familiar as ever, but every month or two they would meet apparent strangers who claimed to have known them years before, not well, but perhaps on a sports team or in a book group. The grieving parents could not recollect them.

Long after their bodies had healed, June and Howard's grief was as sharp as ever, but as the months went by, though the pain did not dull, it did seem to at least recede a little. In addition to their circle of regular friends, they also began to befriend some of those more peripheral acquaintances who would periodically reintroduce themselves. One of them, Lisa, even became their new insurance broker.

And then, one day, completely unexpectedly, they discovered they were going to be parents again. June was pregnant with twins—a girl and a boy. Initially June and Howard were worried that loving the new children would somehow make them feel disloyal to the memories of Deanna and Michelle. But they were pleased to find that after the arrival of the twins—Erin and Eric—the memories of their elder daughters were somehow more present and more alive than before. There was enough love to go around for everyone.

Erin and Eric were a rambunctious, inseparable pair. Like many pairs of twins, as they were learning to talk they also developed an impenetrable language of their own that only they could understand. Sometimes June could swear that they were speaking in tongues, but upon investigation, the twins would prove to be consulting with each other about the best way to flush a teddy bear down the toilet.

One Saturday morning when Erin and Eric were about three years old, June and Howard were cleaning up the kitchen after breakfast. Amid the clatter of the cutlery on the plates, they could hear a mixture of twin babble and regular English coming from the other room where the twins were happily playing. June had just turned off the tap when, clear as a bell, they heard Eric say, "Give me the teddy bear, *Meow*."

Erin replied, "No, *Deedo*—I am playing with him."

June and Howard looked at each other as the blood drained out of their faces. They were speechless. They had never discussed Deanna and Michelle with the Erin and Eric—they were waiting until the twins were older to tell them. They went over to the living room to discover the twins in a quiet but intense scuffle for custody of the teddy bear. When the twins saw their parents, Erin and Eric immediately stopped the scuffle and assumed faces of unlikely innocence.

"What are you doing?" June asked.

"Erin won't give me teddy," said Eric.

"I am playing with him," protested Erin.

"What do you call each other when you're playing with teddy?" asked Howard, as nonchalantly as he could.

The expressions on both twins' faces suggested relief that the dispute over the teddy wasn't going to turn into one of those tedious mediation sessions about "sharing" or some other such nonsense.

"Deedo and Meow," said Erin.

"Where did you hear those names?" asked June.

Erin looked at Eric. Eric looked at Erin. Now there followed a prolonged exchange in twin babble. They didn't seem to be arguing, but if anything trying to reassure each other. Finally, Erin went over to Eric and the two of them held hands. It was really quite sweet.

Eric said simply, "*Those were our names when you had us before.*"

June and Howard at first resisted the idea that Erin and Eric could be possibly be Deanna and Michelle, somehow returned to them. But one day the twins approached June and asked if she would like her watch back. At first she didn't know what her children were talking about, but then she remembered that, years before, Deanna and Michelle had hidden her watch and refused to tell her where it was. She'd been so furious that she sent them straight to their rooms, but they had never told her the hiding place. Now Erin and Eric led June to a bookshelf that positively creaked with dusty tomes.

"The shelves used to be over there," said Erin, pointing. It was true—during Deanna and Michelle's lifetime, the bookshelves had been by the door.

"The chair that you read us stories in was here," said Eric. This was also true. "We crawled in behind it and put your watch in a hole."

June went and got Howard. The four of them piled all the books on the floor and then June and Howard slid the heavy bookshelf aside.

"I don't see a hole," said Howard.

Erin went over to where the wall met the floor and pulled at the baseboard. A segment about a foot long came off in her hand, neatly cut at both ends. It had clearly been filler to patch a gap during some past renovation. Eric went over and stuck his little hand into the rectangular hole that the removed baseboard had hidden. He pulled out their mother's watch and handed it to her.

Soon, the twins also seemed to remember some of their parents' friends. One night after the guests had left, Erin pointed to a faded stain on the carpet and said, "The lady who was here tonight spilled some of her red juice there once."

Sure enough, when Howard and June thought about, it *had* been that very friend who had spilled a glass of red wine in that very spot, much to the dismay of their daughters.

But one person the twins didn't remember from "before" was Lisa, the new insurance broker. Lisa said she had been in a book club with June, but June had lost touch with everyone else in the reading circle and had no way of checking up. Whatever it was, there was something about her that the twins didn't like.

One day, after Lisa had been at the house for a policy update, the twins peppered their parents with questions about her. What did she do? Was she their friend? These and a hundred other questions. When Erin and Eric found out that, if anything happened to their parents, Lisa was supposed to be the person that would bring money to help the twins, they both started shaking their heads and got very upset. They said that it was all a lie and that the money June and Howard were giving Lisa was going nowhere.

A bit spooked, June and Howard looked into it and discovered that the insurance company Lisa worked for had a terrible record of planting loopholes in their policies so that they rarely had to actually pay out any claims. Around this time June bumped into someone else who had been in her book club—the woman didn't remember there ever being a Lisa in the group. Howard and June immediately cancelled their policy and started a new one with a more reputable firm. Erin and Eric were very pleased.

To celebrate their new insurance policy, Howard and June decided to take the twins for the first time to the restaurant that Deanna and Michelle had so loved. They shouldn't have been surprised when Eric and Erin made a bee-line to what had been the family's regular booth.

When the waitress brought June and Howard a glass of wine each, the twins suddenly became very agitated. "No, Daddy," they both said, shaking their heads. "That was the juice you had just before, just before…" They both started to cry violently, their tiny bodies shaking with terrified sobs.

Each parent took a twin and comforted them. As Erin and Eric calmed down, Howard felt sick—had he been drunk when the car accident had taken the lives of his daughters? He couldn't remember.

June seemed to know what he was thinking and reached across the table supportively. "The report said we'd each had about a glass of wine," she said. "We were well within the legal limit. We were not drunk."

Too shaken to eat they decided to just pay the bill and go. Howard asked June if she would drive. She agreed. They strapped the twins into their car seats in the back and set off. June was driving *very* cautiously.

Suddenly from the back seat a familiar tune erupted. The two little voices were singing:

Here we are
In our car
Going far, far, far.

Here we are
In our car
Going far, far, far.

Deanna and Michelle had made the song up. They would belt it out over and over again and wouldn't stop. June and Howard had forgotten all about it until just this moment. Now it was their turn to become agitated.

"Please don't sing that song!" said Howard sharply, turning around to look at the twins.

> *Here we are*
> *In our car*
> *Going far, far, far.*

"Listen to your father!" said June, darting her head around and then turning back to the driving. "It makes it very hard to concentrate."

"Please stop!" pleaded Howard as his memory of the accident flooded back. That song, that song, that ridiculous song sung by two defiant daughters now sung by two equally defiant twins.

June's memories had burst through too, like a midsummer thunder storm, and now she was weeping in the driver's seat, unable to see through the tears. Howard's head was turned back to the twins. The twins had their eyes closed in rapture as they belted out the song over and over again—the song they both knew from long ago, but hadn't sung in so long.

> *Here we are*
> *In our car.*
> *Going far, far, far.*

Between the tears, the singing and the not looking, it's a safe bet that none of them saw the truck.

When the twins woke up in the hospital they knew each other, but no one else. It was as though all memories of their former life (or lives) had been erased. They could walk, talk and play. They enjoyed meeting new people. They called each other Deedo and Meow in voices older than their years. Sometimes they called each other Eric and Erin. Other times they could be heard addressing each other as Deanna and Michelle (which raised some eyebrows, what with one of them being a boy). They never asked about their parents.

Everyone commented how fortunate it was that June and Howard had gotten such comprehensive life insurance.

Ne pas de Fumer

Maggie Rollins loved to smoke. She loved everything about it, starting with rattle of the cellophane, crackling like radio static, as she peeled it off a fresh pack of cigarettes. Then the crisp, promising *shuk* as she slid the central tray out of its surrounding cardboard sheath. Next, the block-shaped sheet of silver metal foil covering the tops of the cigarettes, nestled in the pack like the top of a little sky-scraper. Once the foil was removed, wadded into a tight little ball and relegated to the garbage bin, there were the brown filtered tops of the cigarettes, standing in their orderly ranks waiting for her to choose one. At this point, Maggie always felt the same thrill that she had as a child when she was allowed to take the first scoop from the smooth, pristine surface of a newly opened jar of peanut butter. Having selected her cigarette, she placed it carefully between her lips. Now, she touched the flame of her lighter to the end of the slender white tube and her ears filled with the deliciously parched hiss of the burning tobacco as she drew on the cigarette and sucked down the first lungful of smoke. Then the soothing release as she exhaled the smoke in a beautiful blue cloud.

For Maggie, the length of a cigarette was a reminder of the infinite, for whenever she lit one, she was pleased to think that she had no idea how her world might change by the time it was done. Between the first, sweet intake of smoke and the final exhalation lay limitless possibility. If it was dark, she would hold the stub of her still-burning cigarette between her thumb and middle finger, then ping it away into the darkness, its end spiralling merrily away into the unknown, describing little figure eights, an unravelling chain of glowing red infinity signs.

One day though, between the first puff and the final stub, Maggie's life changed more than she ever could have imagined. It was a cloudy spring day and she was outside for a mid-afternoon smoke break at work. The day's general gloom was offset by the warmth of the winter melt, and Maggie was enjoying watching the passersby on the city street, all of them walking with a relaxed gait, in sharp contrast to the hunched, tense march that the winds of winter always brought on.

As she blew a plume of smoke into the air, it seemed to form itself into a shape reminiscent of a human head and shoulders—a bust made out of smoke—and then it was gone. Maggie tried to do it again, but the smoke just came out in its regular odd shape. She blew a few smoke rings for good measure and then went back inside.

That night at home, Maggie lit her first after-supper cigarette on the couch. And there, by the light of the lamp on the side table, the swirling smoke from her lungs formed itself into the head and shoulders of a man, his eyes sunken and his features emaciated. To her horror she watched as the ghost in the smoke seemed to attach itself to the plume of smoke that rose from her cigarette, as though it needed an umbilical cord to sustain itself. Rooted in horror, Maggie couldn't move, even when the wraith started to make pathetic clawing motions toward her. Then it spoke in a raspy, distant voice: "Join us, Maggie. You are already one of us. Come on over…"

Maggie hurriedly stubbed out her cigarette. The ghost dissipated and she sat there, her heart pounding, tripping over itself in panic.

That was enough to convince her, and the next day she threw out all her cigarettes, bought some nicotine patches from the drug store and joined Smokaholics Anonymous. But, try as she might, it was just too hard to quit, to say goodbye to all those comforting, energizing rituals that made smoking so meaningful and enjoyable to her. It was as though the escape it provided, however brief, was what allowed her not merely to get through her day, but also to move forward with the other things she wanted to do in life. And so, knowing in her mind and heart that she ought not to, but also feeling that she simply couldn't help it, after a week of being smoke free, Maggie went out and bought some more cigarettes.

The horrifying ghost appeared again when she exhaled her first lungful of smoke, and even though she stubbed out the cigarette right away, he lingered there, clawing at her desperately, making beckoning gestures and rasping, "Come and join us," before finally dissipating into the air.

Maggie racked her brain—what could he possibly want? Why did he want her to come and join "them"? Who were "they"?

In the following days, she asked a coworker if he didn't think that the puff of smoke she exhaled looked, however briefly, like a human head. He answered no. So that was it then—only she could see it. As her ghostly smoke stalker clawed and whispered at her to "join us," those around her were completely unaware of what was going on. Well that, at least, was something.

Even though it was expensive, Maggie discovered that the only way to curtail the spirit's presence was to butt out her cigarette as soon as she'd had the first puff. That way, the ghost still appeared after she exhaled but, deprived of the smoke tendril umbilical cord from her cigarette, didn't seem to be able to last long. The other defensive habit she developed was to hold the smoke in her lungs for as long as possible, delaying the appearance of the spectre until the very last moment, then steeling herself and releasing the smoke when her lungs ached and she could hold it no longer. Then the ghost would go through his usual routine for about a minute before gradually dissipating into the air.

A few years went by. Once in a while Maggie would allow herself to smoke an entire cigarette in order to find out what the smoke wraith wanted, but he simply floated there, beckoning futilely to her and saying, "Come on over. Join us. You're already one of us." It was almost as though he didn't want to be doing it but couldn't help himself. But for the most part, she still found the ghost to be so off-putting that she continued on, smoking cigarettes one puff at a time, stubbing them out after every draw and holding the smoke down as long as possible to delay the wraith's appearance.

Of course, as the years passed, the habit of holding the smoke down took its toll on Maggie's lungs. One morning she woke up feeling as though a vice was crushing her chest. The morning after that, she woke up in a hospital bed and heard her prognosis, which was, in a word, "inoperable." She lingered, briefly coming in and out of consciousness.

The next thing Maggie knew, it was dark and she still felt like a vice was crushing her chest. It was a horrible suffocating feeling, as though she'd never be able to breathe again. But then relief—it was growing lighter, and the scent of fresh air beckoned. Where was she? Maggie felt as though she was floating; she seemed to be in a coffee shop. To judge from the light outside it was about two o'clock in the afternoon—afternoon smoke break time. She rotated effortlessly through the air to find herself looking into the terrified face of a man sitting at one of the tables. He was looking up at her, a twisted expression of bafflement and horror set upon his face. Maggie felt as though she might just drift away, but then there was a sudden tug and she saw that she was tethered to the plume of smoke swirling up from the man's cigarette.

Then, without knowing why and feeling she ought not to, but unable to help herself (though sort of enjoying it just the same), she gestured to the terrified man and spoke as best she could. "Come on over. Join us. You're one of us already."

Spirit Guyed

Ed Nougat's heyday had been in the late 1970s and early 1980s, first as the barely competent rhythm guitarist for a band called Spirit Guy, and later as a solo artist with a more than competent knack for writing bubble-gum metal AM radio fodder that appealed equally to no one in particular and so was instantly recognizable to anyone. He became very rich. With his fortune firmly established, Ed went out on tour for several months of every year, playing '80s nostalgia shows and resolutely putting out albums, each one more like the last. The rest of his time he passed on his country estate, called Nevermore.

Nevermore was a conservationist's nightmare and a big game hunter's dream. Ed's property was extensive, but his favourite place to hunt was an area he had dubbed the Whacky Woods. Here, there were many animals to hunt: deer, moose, bears and even the occasional mountain lion. The walls of his house were bedecked with the plaque-mounted heads of the many animals Ed had killed with his trusty crossbow. The crossbow fired arrows that were not merely feathered sticks with pointy ends, but rather short range, laser sighted missiles with exploding tips—they were designed to inflict as much pain as possible, blowing off a limb but leaving the head intact for wall-mounting. Ed had explosively maimed more creatures here than he would have been able to remember, had their heads not hung from his walls.

But even into the brightest life a little rain must fall, and one year, a couple of months before hunting season opened, Ed's guide, a big man known as "Good Time" Bob, died after a long life spent showing others how to kill animals for sport. Despite owning his property, Ed didn't know it that well, spending as many months as he did out on tour, and that was why he needed a guide such as Bob had been: knowledgeable about both the area and its fauna.

Ed was out touring for the summer and early fall, so he got his assistant to interview possible replacements. By the time the tour was over and Ed had returned to Nevermore, he was told he had hired a local Cree man named Grey Bear. Grey Bear was about 60 and had lived in the surrounding area for his entire life. He knew the land like the back of his hand and all of the animals one might encounter in it. And so it was that, on a cool November day, Ed Nougat and Grey Bear found themselves sitting motionless as the sun came up, waiting for a moose or a deer to happen by.

"Before you dubbed this land the Whacky Woods, my people called it the Unforgiving Forest," said Grey Bear without moving.

"You call it what *you* want," said Ed without moving his jaw, "and I'll call it what *I* want."

"My people have hunted here for generations. We hunted only for food and clothing and necessary tools we could fashion from bone. We did not take more than we needed. Have you asked yourself, Mr. Nougat, how much you actually need?"

"I don't *need* to hunt, Chief," said Ed, "but I *do* what I *want*, and what I *want* is to blow the legs off a nice little white tail deer and then mount its head to my wall."

"Payment is required when you kill an animal," said Grey Bear. "In an ordinary forest you would simply offer a prayer of thanks, but the Unforgiving Forest demands more."

"Like what?" snarked Ed. And then, eyeing Grey Bear belligerently, "A human sacrifice?"

"My grandfather would offer up a strand of his hair, a bit of blood or even a few flakes of skin. Anything of himself that he could give back to the Unforgiving Forest in return for the life he was about to take."

"Look, Chief," said Ed. "I do what I *want*, not what I *need*. I don't *need* anything, but I do *want* to catch a white tail deer. We've been here for four hours and haven't seen so much as a footprint. If Good Time Bob were here, I'd have bagged one already and be heading home for breakfast, so if this is the kind of guide you are, I think you and I had better reconsider whether you work for me or not."

"Fine with me," said Grey Bear, standing up and walking off through the forest.

"You're fired!" called Ed unnecessarily.

And then he was alone in the Unforgiving Forest, along with his crossbow and a quiver full of explosive arrows. After a couple more hours of sitting still, Ed realized that no animals were coming by and decided to head back to the Nevermore lodge. By this time it was noon and the sun was directly overhead. Ed, not much of an outdoorsman, was more accustomed to navigating a stage of pyrotechnic explosions than a forest full of trees that all looked the same; he had no way of knowing what direction he was going. By the time the sun was sinking, he had started to panic and began to frantically run through the forest rather than sensibly staying put and waiting for someone to find him.

Soon the dense tree branches were tugging at his impractically styled hair. He had scraped the skin off the palms of his hands in two bad falls. And his shins were bloodied from several hours of clumsy tripping and stumbling as he rushed through the woods. It was in this way that the Unforgiving Forest extracted from Ed Nougat the offerings he was unwilling to give—blood, skin and hair. Armed with these keys to its quarry, the forest began to work its magic on the unrepentant hunter who killed for pleasure and not out of need.

It was when the sun had gone down that he felt the first sear of intense pain and found himself lying face down in some leaves. Had he blacked out? The last thing he could remember was a burning pain near his ankle—was it broken? He tried to stand up and fainted from the pain. When he came to, he reached down and passed out again when his fingers touched the exposed bone at his ankle—his foot was gone! Had he stepped in a trap? Had an animal gotten him and he hadn't known it? Then he felt another plunging stab on his other foot. Now it was gone too and he was losing blood fast. He was in indescribable agony. If Grey Bear had been there, he could have told Ed that he was being subjected to the death pains of every animal he had ever killed. But as it was, Ed Nougat died as he had lived—in ignorance. And as he had taken so many lives, so did Ed's life end—in a welter of pain, with darkness closing in, scared as hell.

Who's Haunting Who?

When five-year-old Elsie Lambeth and her parents moved into their new house, they were all delighted. It wasn't a big house, but it was just big enough for two grown-ups and a little girl. The house was on a pleasant, tree-lined street surrounded by other houses, all built in the 1930s. When the family moved in, the house had been empty except for a mirror, cracked into three pieces and resting in a red wooden frame that looked as though it had itself been broken at one point and was now mended back together.

Elsie immediately took a shine to the red wooden frame and the mirror inside it. So her mother and father found a special glue to stick the pieces of mirror back together and hung the battered but cheery antique up in Elsie's room. Every morning Elsie's parents marvelled at the fact that their thoroughly modern little girl liked to dress herself reflected in this relic from another time. One morning she told them that she could also see a nice old lady in the mirror. Elsie had recently lost her grandmother, and her parents assumed that the visitor in the mirror was some sort of childish coping mechanism. And when Elsie further explained that the nice old lady had a dog and a cat with her, as well as a parrot sitting on one of her shoulders, the parents smiled to one another—Elsie had been asking to get a pet for ages.

Tish Carberry had lived in the little house for her entire adult life. She had lived with her parents until her wedding day, and then she and Harry had moved into the little house that soon became a home. Tish and Harry assumed that, with the arrival of children, they would need a bigger house one day, but as the early years of their marriage went by, no children arrived. Then the war came, taking Harry with it and returning him, miraculously unharmed, when it was over. They settled into middle age, still living in the same little house.

They got pets to fill the empty space. First came a parrot named Polly, taught by Harry to say a string of mildly naughty words (much to Tish's chagrin). Years later they got a cat called Cleopatra, and after that, a dog named Archie. A few years after they got Archie, Harry died, leaving Tish with their pets, still living in the little house they had bought together all those years ago.

The friendly personality quirks of the animals filled Tish's days, starting in the morning when Archie would put his front paws on the side of the bed, cock his head at her and give a little *woof*. Even before she had opened her eyes, she could feel the mattress sink down slightly where Archie put his paws. Then she would roll over and greet the big slobbering dog with a ruffle of his head. Next, Cleopatra would rouse herself from where she slept under the blankets, usually between Tish's feet, and creep forward, a moving lump eager for a bit of playful wrestling. Finally Tish would get up and go over to Polly's cage, and upon removing the towel draped over the cage to put the bird to sleep, was greeted by Polly's raucous shriek, "Good morning. I see Tish. I see Archie. I see Cleopatra. Good morning!"

That comfortable companionship made it all the harder when Archie grew so old that Tish eventually had to have him put down. Cleopatra followed soon after, and then it was just Tish and Polly. Every morning when Tish uncovered the cage, Polly still squawked, "Good morning. I see Tish. I see Archie. I see Cleopatra. Good morning!"

Then one morning as Tish lay there, she felt the mattress move just the way it had when Archie had put his paws on it, and she heard a quiet *woof*. She turned over in the grey light of the dawning day and saw...nothing. She wrote the incident off to her imagination, but the next morning as she lay there quietly, she felt the familiar movement of Cleopatra between her feet. She looked down to the foot of the bed and this time, there was no mistaking it, there was a cat-sized lump under the blankets, playfully making its way up. She played with the lump, swatting it gently as phantom cat paws punched back under the blanket. Then, suddenly, Tish pulled back the blanket to see...nothing.

But every morning, and soon at other times throughout the day, Archie and Cleopatra came to visit her—she might hear the click of Archie's claws on the linoleum of the kitchen or the all-too-well-known *tack-tack* of Cleopatra clawing the drapes. And right about this time, Polly started saying new things, which was odd because Tish hadn't taught Polly any new words for years.

"I see them! I see them!" Polly would screech. At first Tish thought Polly simply meant she could the spirits of Archie and Cleopatra, but then Polly started to actually describe what she was seeing. "Small man at the mirror!" she would say. Other times Polly would shriek, "Lady at the mirror!" or "Big man at the mirror!"

Tish would look over at the old broken mirror that she and Harry had found in the basement when they moved in. They had both liked it, so they had taken the broken frame and shards of mirror and affixed them to one wall as a sort of piece of art. Their friends had regarded it as junk, but

Harry and Tish liked it; for them it represented one of the first choices the two of them had made together when they were decorating their home.

Then one morning, not long after Polly had begun squawking over and over that the small man/lady/big man was at the mirror, Tish went downstairs and could only stare uncomprehendingly—the bits of red frame and had been taken off the wall and somehow reassembled, and the repaired frame now leaned against the wall. She wondered if, as well as the spirits of her pets, perhaps Harry had returned and was responsible for this new mystery. But no—then Polly would have said, "I see Harry," or "Harry at the mirror," or she might even have uttered one of those naughty phrases that Harry had taught her and that she used to repeat when company was over, much to Tish's embarrassment.

This saddened her—if her pets could return, why not Harry? She missed him. Then she recalled that, even though Harry's limbs had been intact after the war, Harry himself was never really the same afterward—he was broken and scarred, not at all the fun-loving helpmeet he had once been—as if his spirit was truly broken, somehow absent, even though Harry's body was present.

But Tish's sadness turned to horror as, one by one, she caught glimpses of the people that Polly could see. It was a cloudy day and she had just been playing a ghostly game of fetch with Archie, tossing one of his favourite balls and then watching it float back through the air with Archie's familiar bouncy gait as she savoured the sound of his toenails on the floor. It was about noon and she hadn't turned on any lights. The gloom suddenly deepened and, looking up, she saw a dapper, middle-aged man with his hair slicked back, dressed at the height of fashion for the 1930s—he was frozen, his hands on one of the mirror shards. She blinked and he was gone, but Tish knew what she had seen.

The next day she'd been playing with Cleopatra's ghost under the blankets of the couch when she looked over again and this time, saw a beautiful but hard woman in her thirties, also dressed at the height of style 70 years ago and also frozen, seemingly attempting to prize a piece of the mirror off the wall.

The next 24 hours were among the most frightening Tish Carberry had ever known. She awoke that morning to find that Polly had passed away during the night. Polly had been about 30 years old when Tish and Harry had bought her after the war, meaning that she and Tish were about the same age. Tish couldn't help but wonder if she would be next. It was another gloomy day. She descended the stairs and froze halfway down—this time there was a large, handsome man in shirtsleeves and suspenders frozen in the act of trying to prize the third shard of mirror off the wall. She blinked and he was gone.

Then she heard the spectral voice of Polly just behind her screeching, "Trying to get in. They're trying to get in. Mirror is a door. Mirror is a gateway."

She spun around on the stairs, but Polly was, of course nowhere to be seen. There was also a quiet *woof* and a plaintive *meow* from somewhere nearby, though Tish couldn't say from where.

Determined to get to the bottom of the mystery, Tish spent the afternoon at the library, pouring through old deeds and newspapers, and slowly pieced the mystery together. Before she and Harry had bought the house in 1936, its first owners had been the three adult children of a once wealthy family fallen on hard times. Bequeathed by their parents to all three of them, the little house had been the only thing left of a mighty fortune. The three siblings were all exceedingly vain and felt entitled to the finer things in life, but they were not really equipped to get jobs. Not content to simply live in a house that was paid for, they had run up staggering debts buying fancy clothes and trying to marry into a family moneyed enough to restore all or one of them to his or her former glory.

In 1935, just before Tish and Harry bought the house, the three siblings had each sued the other two in an attempt to gain sole ownership of their home. Each one swore they would never leave. And then one night, as all three were preparing to go out on the town, they got into an argument over who got to stand in front of the mirror as they primped and preened. In the ensuing fight, the mirror had been broken and the three of them had slashed each other to death with the shards of glass.

That night, after she got home, Tish thought carefully about what she had learned from Polly's posthumous squawking and at the library—the three siblings were almost certainly trying to reassemble the mirror because it represented some kind of portal into the house for them—they wanted to take possession once again. Just as she came to this realization, there was a crack of thunder and the lights went out, plunging the house into darkness.

With the first flash of lightning she saw the "small man" with a shard of mirror in his hands; with the second she saw the "lady" at the red mirror frame where it rested against the wall, stooped over beside her brother, trying to work the pieces back into their frame; and the third flash showed her the "big man" now bent near his sister and brother, desperately trying to wedge the third shard of mirror into the frame. Then Tish heard a savage bark and saw in the next flash of lightning, Archie snapping with his jaws at the arm of the small man; there was a hiss as the next flash showed Cleopatra scratching and clawing at the lady, followed by a camera-flash image of Polly squawking and pecking at the head of the big man.

Bolt by bolt, flash by flash, the lightning lit up the scene like snapshots from a nightmare—Archie, barking, biting and growling, vanquishing the small man forever from territory that was his; Cleopatra, scratching and hissing, tearing the face of the lady to shreds, banishing her from a house where there was only room enough for one regal feline personality; and finally, Polly, flapping, shrieking and clawing at the big man, showing him that if there was going to be any primping and preening done in this house, Polly would be the one doing it. Finally, the three sibling ghosts seemed to burst into glowing dust and suddenly it was quiet and dark—the thunder and lightning had ceased—now it was just the soothing lap of wind and rain.

Tish could feel her pets around her, hear them panting, purring and squawking. She could see them now too. There was Archie, his tongue hanging happily, a string of ghostly drool dripping from his jowls; Cleopatra, insistently, forcefully driving her head into Tish's open palm; and Polly, sitting on her shoulder, playfully nipping at her ear. Only then did Tish realize why she could see them now—she had joined them. Her body lay on the couch and her spirit was now the keeper of the house, along with her pets.

She looked up to see a familiar figure standing in the doorway.

When Elsie told her parents that the nice old lady in the mirror (whose name was Tish) had a nice old man with her (whose name was Harry), they smiled indulgently and marvelled at their daughter's vivid imagination. For Elsie's part, she loved her visits with Tish and Harry, and their dog and cat and parrot. They told her how things had been once— how telephones had wires and hung on the wall; how they listened to radio instead of watching TV; how much a handful of candy cost at the store. And they told her how dearly they loved her and how they would always be there for her as long as she wanted to see them and how they wished they had had a little girl like her, but they were so glad they were friends with her now and would be able to watch her grow up in the house where they had once lived.

Finally, Elsie convinced her parents to get a pet. She chose a beautiful little tortoise-shell kitten. Her parents were utterly baffled as to why she wanted to call the kitten Cleopatra.

Buried Dead or Alive

As the earth shook and the lights went out, the men knew they were at the heart of every miner's worst nightmare—a cave-in. When the choking, terrifying, heart-racing adrenaline of the collapse passed, Al Diguer, the foreman, realized he was still alive and, amazingly, uninjured. His first thought was how dark it was—darker than dark, so dark that the very darkness seemed to have some tangible substance about it that he could feel touching his skin like a warm bath. With the first hacking cough, he realized that, of course, the air was full of the dust of rock pulverized in the collapse. Al began to move about tentatively, his hands held out in front of him. He promptly bumped into one of his comrades.

"It's me, Al. Who's that?"

"Simon—" Al recognized the raspy voice of Simon Ortega, cut short by a cough.

"Who else is here?" Al asked into the darkness, as firmly as he could given that the dust was making it hard to breathe. A succession of voices answered him back, most choked with dust.

"Rob Vitelli."

"Joe Haley."

"Sandy Grade."

"We're all here," gasped Al, pleased that everyone in his immediate group was at least alive. They stood there for a moment, close together in the absolute darkness, listening to one another uneasily breathing in the thick, choking rock dust. Each man's chest felt as if it were being pressed in upon from all sides. Silently, their thoughts turned toward the claustrophobic reality of their situation—trapped half a mile underground with no light and limited air.

And then another voice echoed out of the darkness.

"Hans van Stratten."

And another.

"Erasmus J. Mooney."

And a third.

"Villem Prue."

The five miners' hearts nearly stopped. The mine they were in was more than a century old. All the local residents knew its history. Hans van Stratten, Erasmus J. Mooney and Villem Prue *were the names of three men killed in a collapse here 100 years ago.*

In other circumstances the five miners might have dismissed the reciting of the dead miners' names as some kind of joke, but the fact was, no one would joke around after a collapse. And what's more, each of the ghostly voices had uttered its name in hardened syllables and cornered vowels unknown to modern ears.

None of the five men said anything. The voices repeated themselves.

"Hans van Stratten."

"Erasmus J. Mooney."

"Villem Prue."

And then together, declaiming their joint presence, "We are here!"

"Who are you?" asked Al weakly.

"Hans van Stratten."

"Erasmus J.—"

"All right, we know your names," broke in Simon testily. "But who are you?"

"We are the spirits of men who died here long ago," intoned the three voices, sounding like a dolorous round of Gregorian chants.

"And you're here to haunt us, is that it?" coughed Rob with more than a hint of annoyance in his voice.

"No," said the voice of Hans van Stratten. "We are here to guide you, for soon you will join us."

"And then," said Erasmus J. Mooney ominously, "you will join our ranks, waiting in darkness."

"When the air has run out and you have come over to our side," Villem Prue said with a rasp in his voice, "your spirits shall sleep in suffocation until they are wakened to haunt future souls as unfortunate as we."

As the men started to scream and claw at the walls, Al knew in the back of his mind that he ought to tell them not to scream, since it would use up their limited supply of air that much quicker, but he was too busy screaming himself to bother.

Frosh Week

Every autumn the freshmen at Guild University wondered if one of them would see the Stovepipe Spectre. Making a handful of appearances every fall, the Stovepipe Spectre was a ghostly shadow that appeared only after nightfall. It had earned its name from its silhouette—a tall, thin man in a stovepipe hat and formal frock coat. In fact, even though no one had ever seen its face, most people said it reminded them of Abraham Lincoln.

The Stovepipe Spectre confined itself to the Gargoyle Gallery, the students' nickname for the carved stone gallery that bound the university courtyard. It wasn't seen so much as glimpsed, eerily making its way around the quad, striding purposefully but pointlessly through the shadows of the gallery, deaf to all calls to stop and always fading away before would-be ghost catchers could reach it. It never tripped the many motion-activated lights that lined the perimeter of the courtyard. One observer said, "It's like that film of Bigfoot, where it's just walking away without any rush, walking away into the woods and that's what's so spooky; it seems like it's oblivious to everything around it and then it disappears."

The mysterious figure had been reported since Guild University opened in the early 1900s. Every year the legend was recounted to the freshmen, and every year a handful of students—freshmen, sophomores, juniors and seniors—reported seeing it, stalking creepily through some distant, deserted and unlit section of the Gargoyle Gallery. It had gradually become part of the university's identity, with the university newspaper even being renamed from *The Gargoyle* to *The Stovepipe* sometime in the 1950s.

But this year was different. This year, a young freshman named Charlie Isakov had been walking across the court-yard one night, hand-in-hand with his girlfriend of less than a day, when he spied the famous figure moving silently through the gallery. Charlie shouted and, letting go of his girlfriend's hand, gave chase. According the girlfriend, a young woman with the unlikely name of Elspelina Jasper, Charlie had run toward the gallery, but as he did so, she saw the spectre fade away, dissolving into the darkness. Meanwhile, Charlie had reached the spot where the ghost had been, setting off the motion-activated lights just in time for Elspelina to watch in horror as one of the massive stone gargoyles perched overhead suddenly detached itself and fell straight down onto Charlie, crushing him bloodily beneath its immense bulk.

Elspelina, also a freshman, was not one to let tragedy stand in her way, and by the following week she was dating someone new. One night, crossing the courtyard with her new beau, Elspelina saw the familiar silhouette gliding staidly through the gallery, a column of black on a back-ground of such inky darkness, she wasn't even sure if she'd seen it. Elspelina and her new boyfriend watched and waited until the figure reached the corner and gradually faded away. Cautiously they walked over, and just as the motion-activated light snapped on, another of the massive gargoyles that lined the gallery slammed downward, killing Elspelina instantly. The boyfriend was unharmed.

The second death brought calls for an immediate inspec-tion of the gallery's structural soundness. No cracks, erosion or other structural flaws were found, either in the gallery or in the remaining gargoyles themselves. The gallery was reopened, but people had started to avoid it. And there the mystery might have rested if not for a curious junior and a determined first-year.

Jennifer Poliakoff was a third-year journalism student who had always been fascinated by the Stovepipe Spectre and was frustrated that she'd never gotten to see it. With the deaths of Charlie Isakov and Elspelina Jasper, she decided that enough was enough and turned her investigative instincts to the case. One afternoon she was sitting in the Guild University archives when she realized that an intent young man about her own age was looking at her over the library table.

"Can I help you?" she asked.

"Are you the person who's signed out the file on the Gargoyle Gallery? They said it was signed out, and you're the only other person here."

"Well, yes, this is it. I'll be done in a few minutes."

He sat there regarding her silently as she leafed through the dusty old file. She could feel his eyes burning into the top of her bowed head as she looked through the old papers for something that might be a clue.

"Find anything good?" he asked condescendingly.

"What business is it of yours?" Jennifer scowled at him.

"Elspelina Jasper was my cousin," he said, glaring back at her.

"Oh," said Jennifer.

As it turned out, Sid Jasper was a freshman journalism student in the same program as Jennifer, but he'd taken a couple of years off school before starting, so actually, they were the same age. And, Jenn found herself thinking one day, once you got to know him a bit more, he wasn't that much of a jerk. Sid hadn't known his cousin, the ill-fated Elspelina, all that well, but he was curious about the persistent legend that seemed to swirl through the gloomy, gargoyle-guarded gallery.

"Our family has lived in this town for ages," he told Jennifer one day. "There's a family story that my great, great, great aunt, Winifred Jasper, was the cause of a duel between the two stonemasons who carved all the gargoyles for the gallery."

"Really?" said Jenn with an odd feeling in her stomach. "Because my great, great, great uncle *was* one of the stone-masons who carved the gargoyles. He was killed when the other stonemason shot him, but we've never known why."

They looked at each other, not entirely sure what to think.

Off the university grounds, at the public library, Sid and Jennifer were going through hundred-year-old newspapers on microfilm, looking for some mention of the killing. Each of them was sitting at a different viewing station, and Jenn had fallen asleep at hers after staying up late the night before to hand in the year's first assignment. She became aware that someone was rubbing her shoulder—it felt kind of nice. She opened her eyes.

Sid smiled at her from the next station over. "I've found something. It doesn't say that there was an actual duel, but it does say that two stonemasons, both Russian immigrants, had a fight over Winifred Jasper, the daughter of Matthew Jasper, a local merchant. One the stonemasons was killed when the other one shot him. The victim's name was Vladimir Poliakoff."

"That's him," said Jenn, fully awake now. "Does it say the name of the other stonemason, the murderer?"

As she looked at Sid, she saw all the blood drain out of his face, and a look of terror and confusion came over him.

"What is it? Are you all right?" She put a hand on his shoulder and he snapped out of it and looked over at her.

"The name of the other stonemason—the one who shot your great, great, great uncle—was Dmitri Isakov."

"Isakov? As in Charlie Isakov, the first kid to get squashed by a gargoyle and who also happened to be dating your cousin?"

"Seems so," said Sid. "And look, there's an artist's sketch of the two men."

Jenn wheeled her chair over to see. There, on the glowing screen of the microfilm machine, was a drawing of two men. On the left was the murderer, Dmitri Isakov: short, squat and bearded, wearing a soft cap. On the right was his victim, Vladimir Poliakoff: tall, thin and well-dressed for a stone-mason, wearing a long black frock coat and a stovepipe hat.

"Umm…" said Jenn, unable to find words.

"The Stovepipe Spectre is your great, great, great uncle," said Sid with a wide grin.

"What're you so happy about?" said Jenn. "He hates the Jaspers, apparently enough to kill you all by dropping his gargoyles on your heads."

"Oh, right," said Sid.

A couple of hours later they were sitting in the university bar, trying to make sense of what they had learned.

"Here's what I don't understand," said Sid. "Your uncle has been haunting the university for, what? A hundred years? Why should he start killing people now? As far as I know, none of the gargoyles have ever fallen off until this year."

"Maybe there weren't any Jaspers or Isakovs at the university for him to kill until this year," said Jenn over her wine glass.

"You know, you're probably right," said Sid. "I'm not the first member of my family to go university, but as far as I know, Elspelina and I were the first to go to *this* university."

"And there you have it," said Jenn.

"If you're so smart," said Sid, "you got any thoughts on how I might be able to avoid getting crushed to death by a falling gargoyle?"

"As a matter of fact, I do. Come on."

"Listen, Jenn," said Sid half an hour later as they strolled through the courtyard, "I really like you, and any other time I'd think holding your hand would be great, but here in the…in the courtyard of death, I really don't think it's such a great idea."

"Just relax," said Jennifer calmly.

"Easy for you to say; you're his descendant. He probably likes you."

"I have a theory," said Jenn. "I don't think he's out only for revenge."

"Well, what else do you think he's got up his sleeve?"

"I think he wants to live vicariously through one of his relations."

"You?"

"I think I just happen to be the one he has access to."

"Normally I'd say that dead people living vicariously through living people was a bad idea, but if you really think it will help…"

"I think he wants to see a Poliakoff and a Jasper together at last," said Jenn.

"Lucky things were going that way anyway," said Sid, his voice quavering. "Oh geez."

A figure had appeared across the courtyard in the darkness of the Gargoyle Gallery, tall and upright, walking (or gliding—it was hard to tell) deliberately through the gloom. They both watched it, their hearts pounding.

"Vladimir Poliakoff!" called Jenn.

"Oh great, call him out why don't you," hissed Sid. "You are not getting me anywhere near those gargoyles."

"I don't think I'll have to," said Jenn. "Look."

The solitary figure had stopped and turned. It actually seemed to be looking at them. And then—for the first time in a hundred years—it abandoned the safety of the darkness and began walking (or gliding) across the courtyard toward the two young people, rooted where they stood in anticipation and dread. Unhurriedly, and all the more terrifying for it, the figure continued its sinister perambulation, finally stopping in front of the quaking couple. They still couldn't see anything of its face. It just stood there in front of them, a tall, thin shadow.

Finally, Jenn summoned her courage and said, "I am your great, great, great niece, Jennifer Poliakoff."

The figure bowed slightly to her and then turned expectantly to face Sid. He was so scared that he just stood there, his eyes open wide, quaking in his shoes. Jenn nudged him sharply in the ribs with her elbow.

"Oh, and I, uh, I'm Sid Jasper, the great, great, great nephew of, uh, Winifred Jasper," he finally sputtered.

The figure bowed slightly toward Sid as well and then took a step back. Then it reached one arm up and doffed his stovepipe hat respectfully. They saw a strong angular face that might have been carved from stone itself, but was now animated in a pleasant smile. It was such an engaging smile that it was nearly enough to distract one from the hideous wound on the top of his head. The ghost of Jenn's great, great, great uncle continued to smile broadly at both of

164 Campfire Ghost Stories

them, turned and made eye contact with each of them, then he closed his eyes, stood with this hat over his heart, and faded away.

The Stovepipe Spectre was seen no more. No more gargoyles fell on students. The next year, when Jennifer and Sid became the first joint editors of *The Stovepipe*, they lobbied to change the name back to *The Gargoyle*. It seemed more fitting to remember Vladimir's life and work, rather than his murder and ghost—even if no one but the two of them would ever know that.

SubZero Spirit

Lazlo Roman was a rock'n'roll promoter—neither a good one nor a successful one, but a happy one. Lazlo's specialty was booking has-been hair-metal bands from the 1980s. He packaged them into ghastly "Greatest Hits" tours in which several bands would tour together, all on one bill. Each band played only three or four of their most popular songs before the next pack of ageing, spandex-clad rockers took the stage amid a burst of fireworks (that hopefully didn't set fire to anyone's towering head of hairspray). The reason Lazlo loved his job was that he genuinely loved this music, and it was a chance to meet his favourite bands.

"Do you know who I've booked for next week?" Lazlo asked his assistant Amy one day.

"No idea," replied Amy.

"SubZero Spirit," said Lazlo, pouring himself a celebratory drink (his fourth celebratory drink that morning).

"And they are?" asked Amy.

Lazlo was 45. Amy was 22. It always frustrated Lazlo that Amy was too young to know about the music he loved so much. But she knew how to work the computers and was good at that social networking stuff on those sites like MyFace or SpaceBook or whatever you called them. And she seemed largely indifferent to his excessive alcohol intake.

"SubZero Spirit were the best," said Lazlo. "They always dressed up like pirates—heavy metal pirates—and—"

"Why did they dress up like pirates?" asked Amy.

"I don't know, they just did. And their riders and contract stipulations were legendary; they always demanded a big industrial freezer in their dressing room."

"For what? Their heavy metal pirate TV dinners?" asked Amy.

"No one knows," said Lazlo, "but legend has it that the band drank so much vodka that they needed an industrial freezer to keep it all chilled, and that was why they called themselves SubZero Spirit—because they drank all this super-chilled liquor."

"You don't think maybe they were making a word-play on the legend of the frozen ghost?"

"What's that?" asked Lazlo, pouring himself some more vodka—in his mind, emulating his heroes.

"You know that old story. There's this sailor and he jilts his lover so she throws herself into the water and drowns. Wracked by guilt, the sailor signs on for a long voyage, but the ghost of his lover starts to haunt him and she's like this misty vapour and forms herself into a water wraith before his very eyes because she doesn't want to leave him. And because she'll never age, she casts a spell on him so that he'll never age either. So anyway, the sailor starts going crazy because he can't go to sleep without the ghost showing up and whispering in his ear and all that. But finally, the ship sails up to the Arctic and one night as she appears to him, she freezes solid and can't haunt him anymore. Then the sailor asks to get marooned on an ice floe with the ghost so that he can rest in peace at last." Amy looked at Lazlo and wiggled the stud in her tongue, waiting for some kind of reaction.

Lazlo had stopped listening, though. He was pouring more vodka. "I am actually going to get to meet Vince Vendetta!"

"Let me guess, he's the lead screamer?"

"He sure is," said Lazlo.

The next seven days couldn't go by fast enough for Lazlo. He got the contract for SubZero Spirit and went through it with a fine-tooth comb. He discovered that, after all, he was not responsible for supplying an industrial freezer or even any alcohol to go inside it. The band travelled with their own freezer. Wherever they went, it went too. But he was responsible for ensuring that the dressing room had an adequate power supply for the massive draw of the freezer.

"Well," said Lazlo to himself, "they sure do like their booze cold." He bustled around for the rest of the week, preparing, as best he could, to meet his idols. He called an electrician and arranged for a 220-amp service to be installed in the band's dressing room at the arena. And then he sat back and imagined Vince Vendetta inviting him in for a drink from the band's private stock of whatever it was they kept so chilly.

When the band's tour bus arrived at the arena, Lazlo was there to meet them and had insisted that Amy come too. All of the musicians piling off the bus looked like they were Amy's age.

"I don't get it," she said. "Aren't all these guys kind of young to have been stars in the eighties?"

"Vince is the only original member of the band," said Lazlo. "The rest of them died in bizarre refrigeration accidents."

"What do you mean?" asked Amy.

"Well, I guess my man Vince holds the keys to freezer or something, because all the rest of them died trying to get into it. Johnny Revenge, the guitar player, was found frozen to death just outside the freezer, but it was still locked. Stig Riot, the bass player, got crushed between the wall and the freezer and covered in toxic coolant. And Brutus Mayhem, the drummer, was discovered with his veins pumped full of Freon."

And then there he was, descending the steps of the bus in the flesh, Lazlo's hero, Vince Vendetta.

"Wow," said Amy. "He's aged well."

"He *has*," said Lazlo, sounding just as amazed as Amy. And it was true. Vince Vendetta looked no older than he had in SubZero Spirit's heyday—maybe 25 or so.

Lazlo rushed forward, his hand extended. "Vince! Lazlo Roman. I'm the promoter. Everything's ready for you."

"I need everyone to clear the area while the crew unloads the freezer," said Vince.

"Sure, sure," said Lazlo. "And then maybe we can have a drink together?"

"I drink alone," said Vince, and walked over to the truck where the freezer was being unloaded.

Several burly bodyguards ushered Lazlo and Amy away from the area. They stood across the street and watched the crowd lining up for the show. Amy was thoughtful. She kept looking at Lazlo as if she were on the verge of saying something but then seemed to think the better of it. Finally she said, "Don't you wonder what's in that freezer?"

"It's booze," said Lazlo confidently.

"But wouldn't you like a taste of that booze?"

"Three men have died trying to get into that freezer," said Lazlo. "I'm not about to become the fourth. Besides, everybody knows it's got an electric lock that keeps it closed as long as it's got a power supply."

"But you were there when they installed the extra power lines," said Amy. "You know where the breakers and the cutoff are. You could cut the power and open the lock and finally get a look inside."

"I am not going to pry into my man Vince's privacy," said Lazlo. A few minutes went by and then he said, "I have some last-minute paper work to do," and walked off back into the arena where the show was about to start.

Lazlo went straight to the now empty dressing room, used one of the master keys he was entitled to as the promoter and went in. There it was—the size of an outhouse—SubZero Spirit's legendary freezer.

It didn't take him long to disconnect the power, then he watched as the indicator lights on the high-tech lock winked off one by one. Finally he heard the heavy bolt slide back, and the door was unlocked. Lazlo took a deep breath and opened the door.

It took him a few seconds to understand what he was seeing—the freezer was not stocked with the world's finest vodka, but rather, what looked like a green ice-sculpture of a beautiful young woman in an old-fashioned dress with an anguished expression on her face. Her sightless, transparent eyes were the most frightening thing he had ever seen.

Then he felt something crash down on his head, and everything went black.

When Lazlo woke up he immediately peered once more into the massive industrial freezer and saw...nothing. It was empty. To judge from the overwhelming stale freezer bag smell wafting out of the freezer, whatever it was he'd seen before had been in there for a long, long time. There was also a pervasive odour of saltwater and something else... seaweed?

Lazlo realized that he felt sort of weird too, as though his skin wasn't fitting properly. He looked down to see that he was dressed exactly like Vince Vendetta! Immediately assuming some kind of consciousness transference, he checked himself out in the mirror and was relieved to see that, no, he was still Lazlo, but he just happened to be dressed like Vince Vendetta. Hmm, that was strange—the last thing he remembered was opening the freezer and seeing the strange ice-woman thingy.

Gradually he became aware of a low, muted rumble from out in the arena proper—the show was underway already and he was missing it! He dashed down a complicated series of corridors, got lost a couple of times and then, at last, found himself in the darkness at the side of the stage, watching SubZero Spirit, his favourite band ever, as they reached the climax of their biggest hit ever, "Submarine Luv." It was a song about an amorous interlude between a shipwrecked sailor and a lustful mermaid. The song always marked the payoff of the band's pirate personas with explosive blasts from two gigantic cannons wheeled out onto the stage especially for the end of the song.

Whatever had just happened to him, Lazlo was glad he would at least get to see the famous pyrotechnic excess that marked the end of all SubZero Spirit's concerts. The cannons were wheeled out to massive cheers of recognition from the mulleted, baseball cap–wearing crowd, who all pumped their hands in the air, squeezing their fingers into that ridiculous shape that means "I love you" in American Sign Language and looks like Spiderman firing a burst of webbing, but that feels cool to do if you're some guy in a mullet and a baseball cap at a concert. The cannons went off with massive booming and clouds of smoke amid the wailing screech of the guitars.

That was when, through the smoke, Lazlo saw her, flitting about so quickly and so high up in the air that at first he couldn't be sure of what he was seeing. After a minute though, there could be no doubt—it was the frozen green lady from inside the freezer, but now she wasn't frozen. She was zooming around in a glowing cloud of green mist, and when she dive-bombed the crowd, the humid scent of salt-water came rolling off of her.

The audience thought she was some kind of radical new concert spectacle, maybe a holographic projection or a flying puppet or something, specially added to give a bit of sizzle to SubZero Spirit's tired old set list. They cheered every swoop and dive and roared with approval as she shot toward the stage, straight at a rather nervous-looking Vince Vendetta. Then she seemed to yank the very soul out of him, pulling a glowing, green version of Vince high above the crowd.

By this time the crowd was feeling as though they'd certainly gotten their money's worth—awesomely awesome special effects that looked like not one but two flying green ghosts or something. But as it turned out, that was just the warm up. As the audience's gaze landed back on the stage, they saw Vince, frozen at the microphone, pinned under a lone spotlight. And then, before their very eyes, his skin began to draw, tighten and finally crumble like ancient parchment. From behind the flaking, falling skin, his teeth pushed themselves to the forefront in a beaming skeletal grin, a rictus of long overdue death. As Vince's eyeballs shrivelled and rolled back in their sockets, the rest of his bones seemed to shed whatever skin they had left, and finally, his entire skeleton collapsed in a pile of dust—once a human, now an anthill in a perfectly circular pool of yellow light.

At this point the glowing pair of green ghosts swooped low, hand-in-hand over the audience, Vince and his mermaid chick or whatever it was she was supposed to be. Then they soared up, up and away, seeming to pass right through the roof of the venue—and then they were gone.

The audience went crazy. They'd never seen anything like it before. The ones who weren't already on their feet jumped up, and the roar of a sustained cheer filled the arena, going on and on and on, as two generations of metal-heads roared their mindless approval.

From his vantage point in the wings, Lazlo was in absolute awe. Then he became aware of Amy standing beside him, looking rather pleased with herself.

"As soon as you told me about that industrial freezer the band carted around, I thought there might be some kind of frozen ghost in there. Imagine my delight when I convinced you to unlock the freezer, knocked you out and then discovered that I was right!"

"But what were you so happy about?" asked Lazlo.

"Here's the thing," said Amy. "You really suck at what you do—concert promoting. I, on the other hand, could make quite a lot of money at it. So I made a deal with that poor frozen ghost as she was starting to thaw: she could at last claim her lover's soul—in case you weren't paying attention, Vince was her lover, he jilted her more than two hundred years ago, she drowned herself, haunted him just like in the legend until she froze one day and he started carting her around like that—and in return, she had to get you out of my way."

"How?" asked Lazlo.

"Well, I hope you don't mind," said Amy, "but I got her to make *you* ageless. So now you can bound around with this band of stiff-haired, gangly boys for as long as you please. You know all the words to their songs, you know how Vince dressed, how he moved, and you know this audience; you *are* this audience. And I am your promoter."

Lazlo looked out at the cheering crowd. They were still going crazy. The rest of the band was just standing there, still looking in disbelief at the pile of dust that had, until recently, been their meal ticket. Amy was right; Lazlo knew all the songs, all the moves, all the places that fireworks were supposed to go off. And besides, he was already dressed for the part. Now he could feel an ageless sort of energy flowing through him, but whether it was the spirit of the frozen ghost he could not tell. He drank in the energy of the crowd, the expectancy of his new bandmates waiting for something to happen, the quiet confidence of Amy standing at his side.

Lazlo Roman raised both arms over his head and walked out onto the stage. The roar of the crowd grew louder. He walked to the lone spotlight at centre stage as the crowd's cheers shook the rafters. He was home.

Ghostly Tableau

La Costa Trucking wasn't such a bad place to work. Elizabeth kept telling herself that. In fact, several times a day she told herself that, yet each day she believed it less and less. To start with there was Louis, her so-called supervisor, who sat at a little desk just across from hers. But the thing was, he didn't really do much of what you'd call supervising. As far as Elizabeth could tell, she and Louis appeared to be the only two employees of the company. She soon realized that she was just there for show, to "do front desk stuff" as Louis put it, except that there wasn't really anything to do. Louis always answered the phone, which sat on his desk. Elizabeth didn't even have a phone. Her main job seemed to be to smile at the big, burly men who came in with the brown paper bags. They'd smile back at her, hand Louis the bags and then smile at her again as they left. Then Louis would get up and say he had to go to the bank.

The only time she really had anything to do was when either the building super or inquisitive strangers came around, and then she'd repeat the monologue Louis had taught her about how La Costa Trucking was a family owned business dating back to 1968, and they aimed to fill all of their clients' shipping needs in a reliable, trustworthy manner, blah, blah, blah. Louis would sit there and pretend to be on the phone, talking to some imaginary person on the other end. Whatever. It was a job. Elizabeth was smart enough to realize there was something shady going on, but they hadn't actually asked her to do anything shady and, well, a paycheque was a paycheque.

Then one day after she'd worked there for about a month, Louis asked her to go into the back room and get him a file.

Louis was always very polite, and he said please when he asked her and then sat there, waiting to see what her reaction would be. Elizabeth had never seen what was in the back room before, but she'd seen Louis go in plenty of times, unlocking the door with a regular key that he kept with all of his other keys.

"Well sure," said Elizabeth, "but you have the key."

"Oh right," said Louis. "It's this one." He held up one of the keys on his chain and then tossed the whole thing over to her.

Elizabeth went over to the door, unlocked it and went in. There wasn't much to see; it was just a little windowless room with a bunch of metal shelves full of bankers boxes that each had a month and a year neatly printed on their fronts. She quickly found the box Louis had asked for— November 1988—and brought it out to him. Then she went back over to the door, locked it and handed his keys back to him.

He watched her evenly the whole time and then smiled pleasantly and said, "Thanks. It's autumn and my old football injury is really acting up."

"No problem," said Elizabeth. The old "football injury" gave Louis a pronounced limp—Elizabeth suspected that someone had actually shot him in the leg (or maybe it had been a crowbar to the ankle)—but of course, it was no business of hers.

After that first time, several times a day, Louis would ask her to go into the back room and get a box from some year or another. Then he'd take out thick ledger books, go through them carefully, make some notes, make a few phone calls and then burn the notes in the metal garbage can by his desk.

It went on like this until one day when Louis tossed the keys over and politely said, "August 1973, please."

As she always did, Elizabeth walked over and opened the door, but this time she froze—there was a woman standing in there already, her back turned, reaching up to grab one of the bankers boxes—May 1971. She had flaming red hair in a ponytail and was dressed sort of retro, in a nylon blouse and a skirt and knee-high boots. She was frozen there, reaching up toward the box (or maybe she'd just placed it on the shelf). Elizabeth could see that there were far fewer boxes on the shelves than there were now—just 1968 to 1971, it looked like.

Elizabeth turned around and blinked. The grey afternoon daylight fell into the little office. She looked back and the woman was gone, the shelves full once more.

"What?" Louis said.

"I just felt dizzy," lied Elizabeth, and she went into the room to get the file. She brought out the box and set it on Louis' desk. He looked genuinely concerned.

"You all right?" he asked.

"Yup. Just had a dizzy spell there."

"You can take the rest of the day off if you want," said Louis.

"No, I'm good," said Elizabeth. "But thanks anyway."

A couple of weeks later, it was another grey, cloudy day. The grim afternoon light that fell through the office's single window seemed to cast everything in a gloomy, leaden shadow. Louis asked Elizabeth for the March 1979 box. She caught his keys, went over and opened the door.

There was the red-headed spectre again, motionless, her back still toward Elizabeth, wearing the same clothes, but this time holding up a little compact with a mirror in it. The last box on the shelf was still May 1971. It was as though Elizabeth was seeing a scene just a few seconds later than the last time. But what an odd place for the woman to choose to touch up her make-up. Why not just go to the bathroom down the hall?

"You okay?" Louis' voice interrupted her train of thought.

She turned around to look at him. The grey, gloomy room was there just as it always was with Louis at his desk, looking at her, she thought, with slight suspicion.

"Another dizzy spell," she said. "If it's okay, maybe I'll take the rest of the day off this time. I don't feel all that well."

"Sure, no prob," said Louis.

Elizabeth left the office, found a coffee shop and sat and tried to think things through. First, she was clearly psychic or in tune with some cosmic vibrations or something. What other reason could there be for being able to see something that Louis couldn't see? Unless he could see it but was pretending not to. Oh well, she was psychic—there were worse problems for a girl to have. Second, *what* was she seeing in the back room? You generally expected to see ghosts in the places where they died or places that they'd lived or… worked. Third, those boxes with the accounting ledgers in them were clearly records of whatever illegal activity La Costa Trucking was engaged in.

Curious, and having nothing better to do, Elizabeth walked over to the library, went down into the newspaper morgue and started looking through *The Daily Mail* from May 1971. Before long she'd found it: "Trucking Co. Secretary Disappears." According to the article, Cynthia Atkinson, employed by La Costa Trucking, had been missing for over a week and no one knew what had happened to her. Elizabeth left the library determined to get to the bottom of it—maybe if she could get a better look at what was in those boxes…

Unexpectedly, Louis handed her the chance a week later when he left early one day, complaining about the pain of his old "football injury." Only once he was gone did Elizabeth notice that he'd left the door to the back room slightly ajar, failing to close it as he did at the end of every day—he must have been distracted by the pain in his leg. Cautiously, keeping an ear out for Louis' returning footsteps, she crept over and opened the door.

This time there was a lot of blood. It looked as though the woman had been shot in the back. The compact was still clutched in her hand and for the first time it occurred to Elizabeth that perhaps Cynthia—if that was the identity of the motionless apparition on the floor—had been using the mirror in the compact to inconspicuously see if there was anyone behind her. Peering into the compact mirror of the ghostly tableau before her, Elizabeth saw a tiny face reflected in it, caught all those years ago as it crept up behind the unfortunate woman on the floor.

It was Louis, 40 years younger.

Elizabeth spun around at the sound of a footstep, just in time to see Louis, greyer and more wrinkled, but with the same intent look on his face now as in the little mirror, twist the silencer onto his gun and raise it to point at her.

Ungulatus Ectoplasmis

Since 1847, successive generations of students had trod the hallowed halls of the prestigious Uppity Canada College. For the privileged offspring of the nation's wealthiest families, UCC provided a safe haven from kindergarten to the end of high school. And each fall, as the shadows lengthened and the leaves fell, UCC put on one of its famous school plays. The plays were famous among the students and their families because they were sprawling affairs with cast members from every grade.

This year it was an effort penned by Mr. Wilkinson, the drama teacher, grandly entitled *The Great Hunt*. It was a shambles of a play, all about a large party of hunters who encounter ghosts, goblins and werewolves in the course of a perfectly ordinary fox hunt. Aside from its dubious merits as a piece of theatre, the play's main strength was that it provided plenty of parts for the teeming throngs of students who eagerly came out for auditions. Rehearsals proceeded apace and by early November, the sprawling cast had learned their lines, the sets had been built and painted, and now, opening night, the buzz of anticipation was in the air.

Out in front, parents, siblings and fellow students filed into the auditorium and milled around chatting and catching up as they searched for seats. Downstairs in the dressing rooms beneath the stage, the cast readied itself as casts had since 1847; they put on their costumes and make-up, then lined up in front of George. George was the ancient head of a stuffed moose that had hung upon the wall next to the stairs leading up to the stage for the last 165 years. And every one of those years, before each performance of UCC's amateur dramatics society, every cast member would step forward and rub George's snout for good luck. The fur had long since worn off, leaving a gleaming nub of black gutta-percha or whatever sort of primitive plastic had formed the substrate of George's taxidermied proboscis. And tonight, so far, was no different. Amid murmurs of "break a leg," the assembled company stepped forward, one by one, and gave the moose's snout an affectionate rub.

The first act of *The Great Hunt* went off without a hitch. The cast cavorted and bellowed their lines with youthful abandon, and all of the sturdily built homemade ghost, goblin and werewolf costumes served their purpose, offering a dose of whimsy with no real fright attached. The intermission came and went and the audience settled into their seats for Act II. The lights came up on a ghostly tableau in the forest set, the actors frozen, waiting for the action to begin. And then it happened.

Just as the master of the hunt raised his horn to blow, there wandered onto the stage a glowing apparition—a gigantic moose with no head. After the audience got over their initial puzzlement—a glowing moose with no head doesn't really look like much of anything at all—they broke into applause; whatever it was, it was glowing and you could see through it, and that was pretty cool. But they knew something was up when the cast, to this point frozen like statues, all uttered high girlish screams and ran away, scurrying into the wings like so many mice. The glowing moose with no head clambered about the stage on its long, gawky legs, baffling the audience and terrifying the cast (who knew that it wasn't some special effect), and then it simply faded away. After a short pause, the nervous cast was herded back on stage. Act II began again and went off without further incident.

The next night, the auditorium was packed—standing room only. Everyone was hoping for a repeat of the previous night's strange appearance, and they weren't disappointed. This time, even before Act I had ended, there it was, gawkily stumbling through a scene in which the actor playing the fox explained why he *wanted* to be hunted down and skinned. But just before the 16-year-old linebacker playing the fox could finish his dramatic confessional monologue, the shimmering, transparent slab on legs started prancing about with great excitement. It leapt about clumsily, circling the unfortunate fox actor, looking as though it wanted to stomp right through the stage. And then, as quickly as it had come, it was gone. The auditorium burst into thunderous applause. They didn't even care about the play; they'd gotten to see the glowing thing!

The next and final night, word about the glowing headless moose had spread even further. Chairs had been added to every available corner of the auditorium, and the overflow audience were seated in the gymnasium, where closed-circuit TV feeds provided a view of the stage. This time the headless moose appeared just after the curtain went up, gallivanting about as before, looking for all the world as if it were trying to stomp through the stage. It galumphed about, glowing and randomly passing through cardboard trees until someone at the back of the house stood up and shouted, "It's George! He wants his head back!"

The house went silent. Even the spectral moose stopped and made every appearance of trying to look in the direction of the person who had spoken, but failed in this endeavour, largely due to its undeniable headlessness.

Finally, from the wings, the stage manager called, "I'll get it." In a moment she stepped gingerly out onto the stage, bearing George's stuffed head. Not sure what else to do, she walked over to the glowing ghost moose and, after a moment's deliberation, reached out and more or less set the stuffed head, mounting board and all, onto the broad, ethereal shoulders of its body.

Secured there as if by ghostly moose glue, the head sat firmly on the glowing body. Happily reunited, stuffed head and ectoplasmic body then leapt off the stage, did a victory lap around the auditorium to the wild cheers of the audience, and bolted out the door.

The next year, the UCC amateur dramatic society realized they needed a new mascot, but the members were a bit spooked by the idea of having something that had once been living. So they got one of those electronic rubber singing trout that turns its head out to you at the chorus. Once people found out the new good luck token offered no promise of on-stage haunting, they stayed away from that year's play in droves.

Flanders Air Field

It was not knowing that made the days so bad. Every time one of his fellow pilots took off, Luc Laval never knew if he would come back. Of course, it was the same for the others whenever Laval took off on a sortie, but he and all the other pilots agreed that taking off into possible danger one's self was far better than staying behind at the airfield and watching someone else do it.

As the war went on all of the pilots had, of course, grown close. Each day those not scrambled sat and stewed as their comrades flew off to uncertain fates. So long had this been their reality that most of them could scarcely remember who the enemy was—or was supposed to be. Each day brought the possibility that they would never see their friends again.

They all concurred that intermittently cloudy days were the worst, not for flying but for waiting. In the quiet of the barracks, with nerves on edge, a cloud moving across the sun could cast a shadow that seemed like a movement in the corner of the room. In one's peripheral vision these "cloud-dogs," as they were called, gave false hope for a comrade safely returned or, worse yet, were known to cause a sense of "presence" in the room, as though a ghost had flickered through the edge of one's vision.

Laval had discovered that sometimes the best coping mechanism was simply to lie down on his bunk and take a nap (if his nerves would allow it). Amazingly, sometimes he could drift off, and for a few blessed minutes, he was not filled with fear for the lives of any of the three pilots who bunked in the same room with him—Michaud, Liberté and Jones. But sometimes, he was wracked with terrifying dreams of being shot down, conscious for every second of the terrifying plunge to earth. Just at the moment of impact he would wake up with a start, sweating in his bunk, all alone in the quiet of another afternoon. And all too often a cloud passing over the sun would cause the shadows in the room to shift in that spectral way all the pilots hated.

One day, Jones and Michaud took off as part of a sortie at 1:00 PM. Laval knew it would be at least a couple of hours until they came back (if they came back at all), so he stretched out on his bunk to see if he could coax himself to sleep. Before he knew it, he was in the dream—he had been shot through the right shoulder and it hurt so much that he'd lost control of his bowels and soiled himself. His plane was riddled with bullets and filling with smoke and flames. When he could catch a glimpse through the windscreen, the horizon spun sickeningly and he knew his plane was in the corkscrew of its (and his) final descent. Then, as always, there was the earth, jerkily rushing up at him like a badly calibrated film. Finally, the sudden jolt into awareness.

As Laval always did, he found himself raised on one elbow in his bunk, his heart pounding, his skin dripping with sweat. He looked up at the doorway to see Jones and Michaud standing there, looking at him calmly. Laval looked at the clock. It was only 1:30. They weren't due back for at least another 90 minutes.

"Why are you back so early? What happened?" asked Laval, looking at his friends.

They didn't say anything. They just looked at the clock, at each other and then back at Laval. A chill went down his spine. He had heard about this phenomenon; ghostly pilots coming back for one last visit after their deaths, oddly unresponsive. Had Jones and Michaud been killed?

A cloud-dog moved across the room and seemed to break the spell.

"You saw it too, right?" said Michaud to Jones.

"I did," said Jones grimly, sadly even.

"He only took off half an hour ago," said Michaud.

"We'd better tell the wing commander," said Jones.

"He'll think we're crazy," said Michaud.

"You're right," said Jones.

The two of them stood there a moment longer, seeming to look right through Laval, and then walked off down the hall. Laval had just enough time to realize the truth—that the dream had been real and *he* was the ghostly visitor, come back to see his friends one last time—and then, like a light going out, all awareness ceased.

Laval was gone.

Sisters Forever

Joan and Jocelyn Spense were fraternal twins. Joan was blind. Jocelyn wasn't. Neither one had ever married. All their lives they had lived together, and now they had grown old together. The rhythms of their days were as sure as the seasons. Mornings were spent visiting with friends (although they had remained single, Joan and Jocelyn were very social). Shortly after noon there was lunch, washing up the dishes and then naps. Late afternoons were spent reading to one another, Jocelyn from regular books and Joan from the many Braille books she loved to sign out of the library. In the evenings both sisters enjoyed TV, even though Joan couldn't see any of it, or listening to the radio. And then it was time for bed.

Over the years, the two sisters had come to know each other as only twins can. When they went to church, Joan liked to sit apart from Jocelyn because it made her feel a bit more independent, but she could always pick out her sister's clear, ringing voice, always slightly out of tune, during the singing of the hymns. After the service, one of their many friends would ask Joan to join hands so that they could guide her back to her sister, and always, as they drew close, Joan could smell the pleasantly stale lavender perfume that Jocelyn wore because it had been their mother's favourite.

As so often happens to people who are blind, Joan's other senses had become sharpened—at church, if she happened to forget which friend she was sitting next to, as soon as their hands touched after the service, Joan would know— from the contours of the hand, the temperature of the skin, the pressure of the grip and a myriad of other clues she was unaware of even processing. Joan's heightened senses of smell, touch and hearing in many ways made up for her lack of sight.

One day, following their afternoon nap, Joan awoke first as she always did and, as was her custom, got out of bed and walked along the hall toward Jocelyn's room to wake her. But as soon as she crossed the threshold of her sister's room, she knew something was wrong. Jocelyn's lavender perfume no longer smelled pleasantly stale—it smelled cold and dead. As Joan drew closer her heart started to pound—she couldn't hear Jocelyn's breathing, with the soft click at the back of her throat as she snored lightly in her sleep. She touched her sister's hand—it was cold. Joan stumbled downstairs to call 911. Afterward, she couldn't remember much about the call—it was all so hazy.

"I think my twin sister is dead."

"What's your address, ma'am?" asked the operator.

Joan told her.

"How many people are living there?" the operator had asked.

"Just me and her. Please send someone quickly."

"An ambulance is already on the way, ma'am, and I'm going to stay on the phone with you until they get—"

But Joan was so distraught that she hung up automatically and sat on the couch, feeling as though she were crumbling from the inside out. Then there was a knock at the door and a muffled voice calling her name. She vaguely recognized the voice—was it one of her church friends?—and scrambled to the door and flung it open.

"Jocelyn's dead!" said Joan, and then burst into tears.

The friend's touch was also familiar as she put her arms around Joan and held her, then gently led her back to the couch and sat holding her hand. Still Joan couldn't quite place the touch of the hands, but it was familiar, warm and reassuring—so unlike Jocelyn's cold hand—and she started crying again. Joan was glad to have some company, someone, anyone. She was so upset, it didn't matter who.

She realized that her guest was rubbing her hand reassuringly, and gradually she began to calm down. The visitor was wearing some kind of subtly floral scent, fresh, alive and warm like a summer morning—was it lilacs? Joan thought of her sister's pleasantly stale scent of lavender, but didn't feel so sad this time.

Then her visitor began to sing her favourite hymn from church in a bright, pleasing voice—perfectly in tune. Surely she should be able to remember anyone who possessed such a pleasing singing voice, but the question petered out as she heard the siren of the approaching ambulance.

Then the paramedics arrived and it was a bustle of activity and voices. "How many people are living here?" Joan heard one of the ambulance attendants ask the other on the way in.

"Only two, I heard," he replied.

"Where's your sister, ma'am?" asked the first ambulance attendant when they reached the living room.

"Upstairs," said Joan. "First bedroom on the right."

She heard them clambering up the stairs and then there was quiet. She realized she was standing now. She couldn't hear anyone else breathing. The friend must have left with the arrival of the paramedics. Then there were the steps of one of the paramedics coming down the stairs.

"We're going to take her to the hospital and try to resuscitate her," said the paramedic. "Where did her sister go?"

"I'm her sister," said Joan.

"Sorry," said the paramedic gently, "I mean her twin sister—the one who called 911."

"I'm her twin sister," said Joan. "I called 911."

"But when we arrived there was a woman sitting here with you and she looked exactly like the woman upstairs."

Joan blinked and tried to understand what the paramedic was telling her. Before she knew it, she could feel herself smiling, tears of joy running down her cheeks. It was true, then—Jocelyn was gone forever—but not just gone away, gone somewhere—somewhere that her hands were warm and not cold, where she smelled of living lilacs and not stale lavender, and where, much to Joan's relief, she sang in a clear, musical voice in perfect tune.

The paramedic was starting to ask her if there was someone who she could stay with or who could help her, but she cut him off mid-sentence, simply saying, "Goodbye, Jocelyn."

Día de Muertos

Consuela woke up to a day that was dull and grey. She would have preferred to snuggle down in the blankets with her stuffed animals, but she knew her mother would want her to go to school. So she sat up in bed and threw off the blankets. That was when she saw them, passing by in the street below. They walked slowly, without speaking. Breathless, her heart pounding with terror, she crept to the window sill and peered over it at the scene in the street. Through the morning fog, a parade of skeletons was marching past. There were even kid skeletons, walking hand in hand with their mommy and daddy skeletons. Consuela was just old enough to know that, when we die, what's left is a skeleton. Was everyone dead now? What would happen to her?

She watched them some more. They actually looked quite friendly with each other. The mommy and daddy skeletons were helping the kid skeletons cross the street. The kid skeletons all had backpacks—were they on their way to skeleton school? That seemed to be the only answer. As Consuela watched, two of the skeletons even hugged each other and seemed to laugh, and one of them patted another skeleton on the back. It was all very ghostly and sombre, but all the skeletons seemed calm, not angry about being skeletons—they seemed fine with it.

Consuela wondered what she would find when she went downstairs—would her mommy and daddy be skeletons? Trembling from head to toe, she made her way downstairs and peered around the doorway into the kitchen. Thank goodness! Her parents were perfectly normal. They would know what to do.

Her mother turned to look at her. "Honey, what's wrong?" she asked Consuela, seeing her daughter's frightened eyes.

"There are skeletons everywhere outside," said Consuela tearfully.

Daddy smiled gently and said, "Consuela, it's the Day of the Dead today. Don't you remember? Everyone is just dressed up as skeletons."

"But why?" asked Consuela. "It scares me and makes me a little bit sad."

"Well," said Mommy, "remember how sad we all were when Grandpa passed away?"

"Because he's a skeleton now?" asked Consuela.

"Hmm," said Daddy thoughtfully. "More because he's not coming back."

"Yes, we were all sad for days," said Consuela.

"Right," said Mommy. "Well today, people dress up like skeletons to remember their grandmas and grandpas who have passed on and to remember to still love them even though they're not here any more."

"They're skeletons now," said Consuela.

"Sort of," said Daddy.

"So everyone out there is dressed up like a skeleton to show that they love the people who aren't here anymore?" asked Consuela.

"That's right," said Mommy and Daddy at the same time.

Consuela dressed up in her own skeleton costume and so did her parents, and they walked her to school like they always did. It didn't seem so scary once you were a skeleton yourself. It didn't seem so scary at all.

Chicken Soup for the Disembodied Soul

For Angelina Karr, it had not been an easy life, but it had not been an altogether bad one either. True, her husband had died just after the birth of their third child—Sam had been a good man, husband and father—but though she never remarried, she had found happiness in friends, family and a great career running a yoga studio called Karr-mic Yoga. The dreadful pun on her own name not withstanding, the yoga studio had been a great success. And, truth be known, yoga was about the only thing that helped her cope with her three children.

She loved them all dearly, but Richard, Greta and Jim had been a handful as children and now they were triple the handful as adults. Richard, the eldest, far from being the responsible one was always in trouble of some sort or another. Angelina's greatest disappointment in him was that he did not seem to be a good friend; she had watched more times than she cared to remember as Richard, instead of being there to bail *out* his friends, in fact bailed *on* his friends. Then there was Greta, who didn't feel complete unless she was with a man, always the wrong man; Greta had latched onto a string of lovers, each one less inclined to hold down a job than the last, which only bolstered Greta's own general reluctance to get a job herself. Jim, the youngest, made a great show of being a good provider for his growing family but was, in fact, up to his eyeballs in debt; Angelina had always councilled him to live within his means, but even now, it looked as though Jim might be about to declare bankruptcy for the third time. When Angelina looked back at her life with them and her attempts to help them become responsible adults, she found her own words echoing in her ears, repeated over and over again at the conclusion of some crisis or another: "I'll always be here for you."

And now, as Angelina lay in a hospital bed, drawing to the close of a lengthy terminal illness, she was surprised to find herself feeling a sense of relief; at last she would be free of her children. She didn't really believe in any sort of afterlife, but when she wasn't feeling resistant to the idea, she thought that perhaps there were different levels, just as there were in yoga, and that perhaps death was simply like moving up to another level. At any rate, at least she would finally have some time to herself—a breather, as it were, from the trials and tribulations of her family. Nonetheless, as her children dutifully lined up to say their farewells, she found herself saying, as she had a thousand times in the past, "I'll always be here for you."

The next morning Angelina woke up to find herself dead. Floating above the hospital bed, she looked down at the withered shell that the sickness had made of her body and realized that she felt better than she had in years—she was free! She had read somewhere that Winston Churchill once said he enjoyed painting so much that when he made it to heaven, he fully intended to spend a considerable portion of his first million years of eternity with brush in hand, daubing pigments onto the canvas of the infinite. Angelina decided that she was going to spend her first million years on a journey of self-discovery; so long had she been embroiled in other people's problems, she felt that she owed it to herself.

She was delighted to discover that she had some ghostly friends in the hospital—Cheryl, Harv and Libby—who had all died in the same room as Angelina at various points throughout the last year. They had all learned some of the "ins and outs" of being dead but also relished their first taste of "soul freedom," as they began to call it.

Since none of them had ever been, the ghostly quartet decided to visit Paris. Floating over the Eiffel Tower, Libby said that she was thinking of "moving on"—did any of the others want to come? Although they were dead, the four of them could feel that there was something beyond, tugging at their souls, another level altogether from which they could never return to this one—but it was unknown.

"I think I'd like to come with you," said Angelina.

"Good," said Libby. "Now—"

"Whoa!" said Angelina. "Something's happening to me. I can feel it. I'm being pulled back home, back to the hospital or somewhere nearby."

"Uh oh," said Harv. "Before you died, did you tell any of your children that you'd always be there for them?"

"Well sure," said Angelina.

"So did I," said Cheryl. "Now, whenever any of them say, 'Mom, I need you,' you're going to be pulled back."

"What?!" said Angelina. "It was just a figure of speech."

"It's more than that—it's your own consciousness imprisoning itself," said Libby, chasing after Angelina as she started to drift back westward over the English Channel. "Do you want me to wait for you, before I move on?"

"Er...no, you go ahead," said Angelina. "I don't want to hold you up. It's been great knowing you. I'll see you on the other side. Goodbyyyyyeeee."

And with that Angelina felt her soul whisked back across the ocean to crash land in the kitchen of Richard, her eldest son. His head, which had been sunken despairingly in his hands, snapped up as Angelina picked her ghostly body up from the floor and brushed herself off.

"Mom?"

"Yes," said Angelina with a faint air of exasperation. "You called for me, I believe?"

"Er...well...yes," said Richard, "but I wasn't actually expecting you to show up. You're...uh...dead, as far as I can remember."

"I am, but I said I'd always be here for you, and here I am. What can I do for you?"

"Uh, it's Chris." Chris had been Richard's best friend since kindergarten. "He's getting married and he's asked me to be his best man, but I really don't like his fiancée and it's going to cost me a bundle and—"

"Stop right there," said Angelina with a note of controlled menace in her voice, which was considerably scarier for her being dead and all. "Chris has been an amazing friend to you—he tutored you in math, helped you learn to read after your dyslexia was diagnosed and bailed you out of jail when you got arrested for stealing that cop's hat right off of his head. Don't you *dare* do anything less than exactly what he's asked you to. You owe it to him whether you like his fiancée or not, and no matter how much it's going to cost you. Do you understand?"

Richard had never seen his mother like this, not in life and certainly not in death. He closed his mouth, which had been gaping in surprise. He swallowed drily. Then he nodded. "Yes, ma'am," he said, realizing as the words came out of his mouth that he had never called his mother "ma'am" in his life (or hers).

"Excellent," said Angelina briskly. "And now if you'll excuse me, I have to go and meet my friends in Italy."

"Uh…Mom?" asked Richard. "Will you still always be here for me if I need you?"

Angelina stopped and looked at him. She wasn't sure. "Unknown," she said, and disappeared.

Floating over the canals of Venice, Cheryl and Harv were glad when Angelina popped up beside them. Harv had been telling Cheryl that he felt the pull to move on, but he was frightened of not knowing what was there—if indeed anything was there. Cheryl had been trying to convince him that it would be fine, but Harv was still doubtful and now he was resisting his spirit's natural pull.

Angelina listened to them for a bit and then said, "But Harv, remember what it was like when we were dying—none of us knew what lay beyond, but here we all are and it's fine. It's just like my yoga studio—you move up to different levels and usually they're like the last one, but different. Just different."

"I guess you're right," said Harv. "It's like with my paint store; people would come in and want me to tell them what their rooms were going to be like once they'd painted them a new colour, and I couldn't. All I could do was find the paint they wanted and send them on their way."

"Didn't your store have one of those computer systems where you can bring in a photo of the room and then put it in the computer and see what it's going to look like with different colours?" asked Cheryl.

"No, we didn't," said Harv curtly. "You had to use your imagination and have a bit of faith."

"Well there you go," said Angelina. "Imagination and a bit of faith."

Harv looked at them with his ghostly eyes. "Well you two, it's been nice knowing you. I'll say hi to Libby if I see her. Here goes." Harv smiled and with that, he was gone.

"That was lovely," said Cheryl.

"It was," said Angelina. "Say, I was wondering if you wanted to go and see the Leaning Tower of Pisa. I've never been."

"Neither have I," said Cheryl.

"Well good, then we'll just—oh no!" Angelina felt herself being sucked back across Europe, across the ocean, toward home.

She crash landed in her yoga studio. She had left Karrmic Yoga to her daughter, Greta, but it looked as though, in the time since her death, it had really gone downhill. The yoga mats were worn and tattered. The little burbling Zen rock fountain she'd installed in one corner burbled no more and was now a stagnant pool of still, briny water. And slumped cross-legged on the floor beside it was Greta, her head in her hands, weeping softly.

"Greta," said Angelina, gently but firmly.

Greta looked up. "Mom?"

"Yes, yes," said Angelina shortly. "I told you I'd always be here for you just before I died, and so now my spirit is irresistibly pulled back to you when you say you need me."

"That's beautiful," said Greta.

"Not really, no," said Angelina. "What can I do for you?"

"Oh, it's Gunnar—you remember Gunnar—well when you died and left me the yoga studio he promised he'd help manage it, but all he does is sit at home all day in the lotus position meditating. He's completely useless and—"

"Stop right there! When your father died, I sank all my savings into starting this yoga studio and then I worked like a downward dog to support the three of you! I will not stand by and watch while you allow everything I've built to crumble just because you won't do it yourself! Now, listen to me—*you* are going to do the work that you need to do. Not Gunnar, not me, *you*. And the first thing you are going to do is clean out my Zen fountain and plug the damn thing back into the wall! That's all it takes, you know; you just have to try! Just because a door isn't being held open for you doesn't mean it's locked. You just have to reach out and turn the handle. Do you understand?"

"Yes," said Greta in a small voice. She got up rather dazedly, went over to the Zen rock fountain and started scooping the briny water into a bucket. Then she scrubbed out the fountain, filled it with fresh water and plugged it into the wall. Without any additional urging she even got a ladder and replaced the burnt-out light bulb that normally shone down cheerily on the little bubbling cascade. Once her burbling fountain was burbling again, Angelina felt that the feng shui of the studio had been restored and that perhaps her daughter had been able to get a glimmer of understanding about the rewards of work. Angelina started to fade away.

"Wait!" said Greta. "If I call you, will you come again?"

"Unknown," said Angelina, and then she was gone.

Cheryl and Angelina had just arrived at the Taj Mahal when Angelina was yanked back to the den of her youngest son, Jim. After she'd gone through the rigmarole of explaining her situation, Jim told his tale of woe.

"I'm about to declare bankruptcy for the third time and I'm just so tired of feeling like—"

"Stop right there," said Angelina. "You are not going to declare bankruptcy a third time so that you and your family can live beyond your means. If you are tired of feeling bad, then do something about it! Pay off your debts! Your sister is probably looking for some help running the yoga studio. Stop sulking and start doing!"

Jim was gaping at her. "Okay," he said meekly, "will do."

Angelina looked at her youngest son and felt better than she had in years, even since she'd died. She realized that the debt she had felt toward her children—to always be there for them—had been paid in full. She was done.

"Jim," she said. "You're not going to see me again. I love you. I love your brother and sister too. Please tell them that for me. They won't think you're crazy. Goodbye."

Back at the Taj Mahal, Angelina said, "Libby was right—my promise to always be there for my children was imprisoning me. I'm moving on now. Do you want to come?"

"I'm not ready yet," said Cheryl, "but I'm glad you're going. What do you think it will be like?"

Angelina looked at her ghostly friend for the last time and then said, "Unknown."

4
The SALIGIA Cycle

SALIGIA is a mnemonic denoting the Latin names of the Seven Deadly Sins.

Superbia: Pride

Avaritia: Greed

Luxuria: Lust

Invidia: Envy

Gula: Gluttony

Ira: Wrath

Acedia: Sloth

The following, though not in that order, are ghost stories chronicling the consequences of each of the Seven Deadly Sins.

Pride

Carl was a body builder. The most important thing in his life was being admired by other people so that he could feel good about himself. And when he felt good about himself, he felt really good about himself. So good, in fact, that he knew deep down in his heart that his magnificently buff, ripped bod made him better than regular people with regular bodies.

Every morning when he went for his first workout of the day, he admired a statue of some Roman god that sat in the lobby of gym. But even as narrow and ignorant an eye as Carl's could see that it wasn't a very good statue, made as it was out of some kind of cheap plaster that had started to fall off to reveal the wire frame underneath. Nonetheless, he could see that at one time the statue had been hung with solid, beefy muscles. One day he asked the front-desk attendant who the statue was supposed to be.

"Hercules," said the attendant. Then she smiled at Carl and he felt good about himself—really good about himself.

"Thanks," he said, flexed his pectorals for her, and left.

Wanting to find a better statue of this Hercules, Carl decided to try the museum, which he'd always heard about but never visited because it sounded really boring. Carl saw a lot of dinosaur skeletons, but no statues of Hercules. Was this whole stupid museum just a bunch of dinosaur skeletons? Then he went up an escalator and there were a whole bunch of statues and Carl understood: the same way the different kinds of exercise machines were all grouped together at the gym, the different kinds of skeletons or statues were grouped together at the museum.

And there was Hercules—the plaque in front of the statue said that Hercules was only part god, but as far as Carl was concerned, a god was a god. The smooth white marble from which the statue had been carved gave a good sense of full, solid muscle, and Carl thought it was pretty amazing that you could make stone look like muscle. But here was the thing: Carl wanted to be better than some old Roman god. He wanted his muscles to look like they were plastic or something, plastic that was really hard and smooth and ripply. So that was what Carl set out to do—surpass the gods.

That night, Carl woke up suddenly in his bed. He peered around his darkened room and found his gaze drawn to the pitch black of the corner opposite. He blinked several times, trying to make sense of what he was seeing—the statue of Hercules he had seen in the museum was now looming motionless in the corner of his room. He sat up, and the statue melted away into the harmless shape of his favourite white track suit, freshly returned from the cleaner's and draped from a coat hanger hung from a hook on the wall. The blood pounded in his ears with relief, and Carl settled once more back to sleep.

The next day, Carl had a really good morning at the gym and drank his post-workout protein shake right on schedule. When he got to work he was also supposed to eat a small protein-rich meal to further aid the growth of his muscles. He chewed down the little meal of chicken mixed with protein supplements and felt stuffed. This was the only part of being buff he didn't like—how much he had to eat all the time to pack on muscle. It made him feel bloated and full a lot of the time and not like the buff, hard bod he knew himself to be. In Carl's brain, eating a lot all the time somehow suggested that maybe he wasn't better than everybody else, since people who were not buff and hard were always eating a lot too. He realized that in his case, eating all the time helped him to build—well you get the idea of the circular thought cycles going on in Carl's head and why he didn't like having to eat all the time.

That night Carl woke up again and blearily saw another white form in the corner. He knew it couldn't be his track suit this time because he'd worn it to his workout that morning and sweated in it and sent it back to the cleaners. And this time it wasn't the statue of Hercules anyway, it was some other white stone statue, of a guy in sandals and a sort of skirt and metal chest plate and carrying a short little sword—he was a gladiator, that's what he was. Carl sat up and blinked, and this time *the statue moved!*

"I am the ghost of Gluteus Maximus," said the statue, "a gladiator from long ago."

"What do you want with me?" sputtered Carl.

"I'm here to help you achieve your goals," said Gluteus, removing his chest plate.

Carl took a long look at the ghost's physique. Gluteus was definitely fit, but he was thick and even like a tree trunk, not sculpted and ripply like Carl wanted to be. And his biceps were long and even, not bursting through in the shape of baseballs like Carl's.

"No offence," said Carl, "but I want to have a different kind of body than you have."

Gluteus sneered, "In my day, muscles actually had to be good for something—fighting or doing physical labour, not just to fulfill vanity. In my day we had a name for pretty boys like you—Muscle Marys. You've got muscles, but they're not good for anything, and you balk at the slightest hint of

204 Campfire Ghost Stories

actual physical labour. Nonetheless, since you have chosen to try to surpass the gods, the gods have sent me to help you achieve that goal."

Gluteus smiled in a way that Carl didn't like, as though something was making Gluteus very happy, but he knew that whatever it was would *not* make Carl happy.

"What if I don't want your help?" asked Carl tremulously.

"You've got my help whether you want it or not," said Gluteus amicably, and with that, he disappeared.

The next morning, Carl was inclined to view the whole thing as a dream and went about his normal morning work-out routine. Then, as usual, he found himself back at the office, ruing his mid-morning mini-meal of chicken and protein supplements. And suddenly, there over his left shoulder, was Gluteus Maximus, urging him on.

"Eating more may make your body feel bloated and stuffed now," said Gluteus, "but you know it will make you feel good about yourself afterward—really good about yourself."

When Carl heard it said like that, so simply and directly, of course it all made sense. He shovelled down the food he really didn't want because he knew that ultimately, it would help him feel good about himself. And in the following days, whenever Carl was staring down an unwanted meal, Gluteus Maximus was there with a few words of encouragement that always worked.

Eventually, all the ghost of Gluteus Maximus had to do was appear over Carl's left shoulder and simply chant, "More. More. More. More." And when he thought of how it would help him to look buff, Carl forced himself to choke down another of his specially formulated meals. As he strove to surpass the gods, Carl grew ever more muscular and really quite odd-looking as he ceased to have a physique that registered as normal to human eyes.

But he felt good about himself, really good about himself, in spite of the strange looks he was beginning to draw from people. Whenever he stopped to think about the odd looks he garnered and whether they were reason for him to no longer feel really good about himself, Gluteus would appear over his shoulder with the never ceasing chant: "More. More. More. More." And Carl would start to eat.

When Carl didn't show up for work one day, the appropriate inquiries were made. The medics found him sitting at his kitchen table. They couldn't tell whether he had died from choking to death or whether it was the ruptured walls of his stomach that had done it. His gullet and mouth were still full of food, as was his stomach cavity. It was as though he had been unable to stop eating. Investigators were also mystified as to the presence of a Roman breastplate that was well over 2000 years old.

At the mortuary, the embalmer thought to herself that if the deceased hadn't overdone it, he might have been the most physically perfect cadaver she had ever seen. Well, she thought to herself, it didn't matter now—all he was was a body, a buff, ripped body—nothing more. She whistled to herself as she set about draining the fluids.

Greed & Sloth

Teddy and Henry had been friends since childhood, and in all that time they hadn't done an honest day's work between them. They were incredibly stupid, unbelievably lazy and terminally greedy. Too lazy to work or even steal, they passed their days scamming the welfare office, skipping rent and moving into a succession of apartments that gradually decreased in size as they increased in filth.

Every week the two of them scraped together a couple of dollars to buy a lottery ticket. This week, Teddy couldn't be bothered to get out of bed to give his roommate a dollar before Henry went down to the corner store to buy the ticket. As was their custom, whichever one of them bought the ticket would spot the other one a dollar, which was never repaid although it was supposed to be. And so Henry dragged his feet down to the store, bought the ticket and went back to their crappy little apartment.

That was the week they picked the winning numbers and won 60 million dollars. Henry immediately turned on his lifelong friend, pointing out that Teddy had not paid him the dollar for the winning lottery ticket that would entitle him to half of the money. Teddy was enraged and, feeling entitled to the entire 60 million dollars anyway, killed his friend by sitting on his chest until Henry suffocated, since this involved the least amount of effort. He stuffed the body in an old trunk and dragged it down to the curb to wait for garbage day. Then he claimed his winnings.

After his picture appeared on the front page of the newspaper, Teddy figured that everyone he knew was going to start asking where Henry was, since everybody knew the two of them were friends. But in this, as he was in most things, Teddy was completely wrong. What happened instead was that anyone he'd ever met (for the most part, low-lifes like himself) suddenly came out of the woodwork and wanted part of the money. No one cared about Henry, no one even asked about Henry, but they did care about money loaned and never repaid, drinks bought but not remembered and favours done but never returned.

Teddy bought a garish mansion (think cream-coloured plaster with details in gold leaf), shut himself away there and tried to ignore his lawyers, who were constantly hovering around with some new claim on his millions that hadn't a hope of succeeding, but that would have to go through the courts. There was the stripper who had given him bus fare; the bartender who had given him a free drink; and the bookie who had done nothing more laudable than simply pay Teddy his winnings. All of them wanted thousands if not millions of dollars.

One night, as Teddy sat watching the huge TV that was now his most prized possession, the screen filled with static. When it cleared, there was the ghost of Henry against the colour bars. He was unpleasantly mangled, having been put through a garbage truck after his death, but there he was nonetheless.

"Hey look, you jerk," he said to a flabbergasted Teddy, "did you ever think of maybe just sharing the money? It's too late for me, but some of those people who keep coming to you, they really need the money, even though you think maybe they don't actually deserve it. Ever thought of just giving them some?"

"It's *my money*," said Teddy, gritting his teeth.

"Actually it's my money," said Henry. "I paid for the ticket and then you murdered me."

"It's *my money* and I want *all* of it," said Teddy, his face contorted into a feral grimace. "If I've got all of it, nothing can touch me. And I'll never have to work again."

"Again? You've never worked to begin with," said the ghost of Henry. "You're greedy and lazy. That's how we both got here in the first place."

"Being greedy and lazy has worked out all right for me," said Teddy.

"Yeah, well, *you* being greedy and lazy hasn't worked out so well for *me*. What you're going to find out is that *other people* being greedy and lazy eventually doesn't work out so well for *you*."

Teddy clicked the remote several times, trying to change the channel, but Henry's ghost wouldn't go away and taunted Teddy from whatever TV show happened to be on—he pranced ghoulishly across the stage of *Canada Has No Talent*, cavorted behind the judges of *Losers Desperate to Be On Television* and executed a rather gory series of pirouettes behind the contestants on *I Couldn't Care Less Whether You Can Dance or Not*. Finally seeming to tire of his spectral channel surf, Henry departed.

But although Henry's ghost was gone, his words echoed in Teddy's ears. Maybe he *should* just share some of the money. He had always thought that winning the lottery would solve his problems—namely the problem that he didn't want to work but still felt entitled to all the stuff that people who did work had. And it was true that now he didn't have to work and he had all the stuff he wanted, but at the same time, there were all these people trying to get at his money, and he had no one to turn to since he had murdered his only friend (he was only troubled by the murder of Henry when he was feeling lonely).

And so, since it seemed like the easiest thing to do, Teddy tried giving relatively small amounts of money to the people who approached him. Out of his $60 million fortune, he gave $1000 to the stripper who had given him bus fare and $500 to the bartender who had given him a free drink, but nothing to the bookie who had, after all, simply paid him his winnings.

What Teddy had failed to take into account was that everyone he knew was as greedy and lazy as he was; when word got out that he had actually shared a bit of his fortune, the appeals for money multiplied. Letters and lawyers arrived by the carful, each demanding more and more for less and less.

One night, Teddy was trying to forget about everything by losing himself in reality TV shows when once again the ghost of Henry appeared, this time lurking behind a palm tree on *Idiots Not Really Stranded on a Desert Island*. Teddy sat up and peered into the TV screen. Knowing it wouldn't do any good to change the channel, Teddy just sat there glumly, his chin in his hand, waiting for the abuse to start. He watched as the mangled ghost of Henry made a variety of rude gestures at him. He was too dumb to think of simply turning the TV off.

"Well," said Henry, "this is your last chance. If you don't do something, your downfall is going to follow pretty quickly."

"Do what?"

"At this point your only options are to either give away all the money or move overseas so no one can get to you," said Henry.

"The money is *mine* and I want *all* of it," snapped Teddy. "And moving overseas is way too much trouble. I can't be bothered."

"Well, it's your funeral," said Henry. "I tried to warn you."

The next day an angry mob descended on Teddy's mansion. They swarmed the gates, overpowered the guards and attacked the house. All of them were people with no real claim to Teddy's money, but who felt themselves somehow entitled to some or most of it—as much of it as they could get. And all of them were too lazy to go through the normal route of acquiring money, namely working for a living. Forming an angry mob was the easiest thing for them to do. It required very little effort.

They tore Teddy limb from limb.

"Welcome to another ghostly episode of *I Won the Lottery and It Killed Me*. I'm your host ghost, Henry, and this is my murderer and special guest ghost, Teddy. Now Teddy, I won the lottery and you killed me. Then you took the money and an angry mob killed you. How do you think being greedy and lazy figured into your demise?"

"Well Henry," said Teddy, "you and I have known each other a long time and let me tell you, I still want that money and I still don't want to have to do anything to get it."

"You must be frustrated that there are no possessions after death and yet the forces of the afterlife compel you to go through the effort of being on these talk-shows."

"I sure am, Henry. Other ghosts ask me if I've learned my lesson, and I tell them I don't think there was any lesson to learn. I'm still greedy and lazy and I always will be."

"For eternity," said Henry.

"For ever and ever," said Teddy.

Gluttony

In 1847, the ill-fated Mead Expedition sailed off to the Arctic on what was supposed to be a voyage of scientific discovery. Led by the notoriously strict Jonas Mead, the expedition of 50 hardy men set forth in a single ship, the *Trencher*, loaded with enough food and supplies to endure at least three harsh Arctic winters.

But as the years went by, there was no word from either Captain Mead or any of the crew members. It wasn't until seven years later, in 1854, that another Arctic exploration vessel, the *Bulwark*, came upon the *Trencher*, adrift amid the ice floes. The *Trencher*'s crew was all dead, their faces frozen into expressions of horror. The eyes of each man were open, clouded and frozen like white marbles transfixed by some unknown terror. Their lips were drawn back either through fright, cold, rigor mortis or all three, exposing the corpses' teeth in long-dead snarls. The *Trencher*'s enormous supply of food was largely intact, the crew apparently having consumed only as much as the outward leg of the journey would have required. It was difficult to tell what had killed the crew, but the best guess was fear.

Upon reading the *Trencher*'s log, the crew of the *Bulwark* learned that one man, Edward Salk, had been marooned for stealing food from the ship's stores. This is his story.

Edward Salk knew he oughtn't sneak food that might be needed later, but having grown up on the streets of London in the 1830s, he also knew that you took food where and when you could get it—and here was a whole ship's hold-worth of salted pork and hardtack. At first he only snuck a few bits of hard ship's biscuit, softening the rocky mouthfuls with his spit before chewing them up and swallowing them. He wasn't actually hungry, but it was food and it was available and he wanted it. Soon, Salk had moved on to the precious salted meat that was key to the survival of the crew, and that was when he got caught. Captain Mead marooned Salk on a little speck of land dubbed Hunger Island. The *Trencher* sailed away. Edward Salk died horribly from starvation.

When Salk's ghost awoke from his body, it was not merely hungry, but ravenous. And now, in his ghostly heart, Edward Salk knew that his disembodied soul craved not bread and meat, but horror and panic. In short, Salk now fed on fear itself. The duration of his afterlife would depend on a steady diet of other men's anxiety and terror. Floating high above the grim Arctic waters, Salk's ghost espied his meal ticket, in death as in life: the *Trencher*.

When he materialized in front of Captain Mead, Salk savoured the other man's fear, confusion and terror and then sucked it out of him. Captain Mead collapsed, dead from shock. The ghost of Salk felt sated, but when the first mate and the bosun came upon the captain's body, the scent of their fright was more than Salk could bear and he quickly scared them to death as well, now feeling glutted on a delicious surfeit of anxiety, alarm and apprehension.

The ghost of Edward Salk slapped his belly and uttered a satisfied belch of undigested worry. It would be several days before he would need to feed again. If he rationed himself wisely, perhaps the crew might eventually decide to turn the ship back and he could feed on their terror until the

Trencher reached a settlement, where further supplies of deathly fear were sure to be plentiful.

At least that was Salk's plan. He hadn't counted on the appetizing spikes of intense fear and shock when the surviving crew discovered their dead shipmates. In less than a day, Salk had scared the entire crew to death and floated woozily over the ship in a sort of ectoplasmic food coma.

It was at this point that Salk realized there were no more frightened souls for him to feed on. How would he survive? First he felt a prick of surprise and then a stab of worry. What would become of him? As he realized what he had done, Salk's worry blossomed into full-blown panic. And although he was already filled with fear and terror, scarcely having room for more, Salk's gluttonous soul instinctively began to feed on his own fear, gobbling away at him from within until all that was left was the ship of floating corpses.

Lust & Envy

When Randy first set eyes on Virginia, he wanted her more than anyone or anything else. So he asked her out on a date, she said yes and that was that. The next few months were perfect, as far as Randy was concerned. He thought about Virginia all day—her smiles, her sighs, the warmth of her skin, the urgency of her embrace—and then he got to go home to her. He was so consumed by his desire for Virginia that he lost a succession of different jobs: he crashed a truck into a lamp post when she jumped into his thoughts and he forgot to turn; a memory of her the night before caused him to lose his place on a production line; he lost his job as a retail clerk when she so filled his thoughts that he was unable to learn how to use the cash register.

But at the end of the day, it didn't matter because Randy got to spend the night with Virginia. For him, each night's passions fuelled the next day's distractions. Tempting visions of Virginia ignited his desire the moment he left her in the morning, and blush-worthy memories fanned its flames throughout the day. She was all he could think about, all he would think about, all he cared to think about. Randy even shut out his friends, so intent was he on spending as much time with her as possible and so unwilling to even try to pull himself away from the addictive nature of his perpetual thoughts *about* her and overwhelming physical desire *for* her.

After about three months of this, Virginia woke up one morning feeling as though she had been away on a long trip and life back home was beckoning. It wasn't that she wanted to end the relationship with Randy, far from it. But after three months of surrendering her person and personality to the entity that was "the couple," Virginia understandably felt the need to reassert a bit of her individuality.

First, she suggested they take a night off, their first apart since they'd started dating. Randy was actually all for it; he thought being apart from her for one night would build his desire to a fever pitch and make their reunion that much more explosive. And indeed it did.

Then, about a month later, Virginia told Randy that she wanted to go away to Montreal for the weekend with a couple of girlfriends. As before, she in no way wanted to end the relationship, but she needed some time for herself and in the company of other people. Unfortunately, this was where things turned a corner for the worse.

At first, Randy was fine with this plan—after they'd spent the night apart a month earlier, their return had been heart-poundingly thrilling. But this time, almost as soon as Virginia and her friends had pulled out of the driveway on Friday night, Randy's imagination went into overdrive—not because he was looking forward to her return, but because all he could envision were the suave French Canadian men she might meet in Montreal and how she might choose to be with one of them instead of him or how she might have a brief affair with someone before returning home to him as though nothing had happened. Surely if she didn't want to spend every minute of every day with her attention focused solely on him, then something must be the matter—she must be tiring of him.

These thoughts, combined with her brief absence, made his desire for her even stronger, actually painful. By Saturday evening, Randy was already haunted by the memories of how he and Virginia *had* been when they were together, not giddily anticipating how they *would* be.

By the time Virginia returned on Sunday night, any relationship they might have had was doomed by Randy's slow but sure descent into paranoid madness and suspicion. It wasn't long before Virginia actually did leave Randy, and although he made a great show of saying good riddance, he was haunted more than ever by desire for her and by unwelcome but uncontrollable memories of her breath in his ear and the touch of her hand on his chest. When he learned a few weeks later that she had found someone new, all three of their fates were sealed.

Randy was consumed with jealousy made all the worse by fragmented memories of being with her and the never-absent ache of still wanting her. Sometimes he would imagine Virginia with her new lover, and his brain felt as though it would explode even as his stomach churned sickeningly. It was these unwelcome, intrusive thoughts of her with someone else that truly made him go mad: the notion of her smiling at another as she had smiled at him; sighing for another as she had sighed for him; enfolding another as she had enfolded him. A couple of weeks of this was more than Randy could bear, and he knew what he wanted to do about it.

After it was done (how and where and when aren't important), Randy felt better for a few days. The two of them were gone for good. But then one night, Virginia and…what was his name? Had Randy ever actually known his name? Well, it didn't matter now. Virginia and her lover appeared in Randy's bedroom one night, ghostly and glowing. She looked lovelier than ever, with her shimmering skin. Her lover looked pleased, as though at last he finally had her to himself. They stood there, holding hands and looking directly at Randy. Then they turned toward each

other and began doing things that Randy had never suspected ghosts could do.

Randy heard each ghostly gasp and saw every quiver of
ectoplasmic ecstasy. Even when he closed his eyes he could
see fragmented images—eyes closed, lips parted, shoulders
bent. And when he opened his eyes they were still there,
each one occasionally looking over to make fleeting eye contact with him before returning to their ghostly writhing.
Randy rolled onto his back, but they appeared floating in
mid-air over his bed.

Only now did it dawn on him that they were ghosts—
they would never die, and he was going to be haunted by
them for the rest of his life and probably after his death too.
He closed his eyes again but there they were, Virginia looking as beautiful as ever she had in life, making him want her
again, but reminding him that even in death she had given
her heart to another.

Wrath

Ira Verge was close to retiring. In his years as an elementary school teacher, he had earned himself a reputation as one of the meanest there was. Decades of complaints from angry parents and tearful kids had all run up against the powerful teacher's union, compelled to stand behind their member even though none of Ira's colleagues would have wanted him to teach *their* kids. It didn't help that all of the other teachers at the school were women—Ira's harshness would have stood out anyway, but the fact that he was a man surrounded by female peers only threw his explosive temper into sharper relief. But Ira was heading into his final teaching year. And after countless interventions, courses in anger management, empathy training and kindness counselling—all to no avail—Ira's colleagues had decided to suck it up for one more year. Parents whose children were unfortunate enough to be in his class steeled themselves for a tough year.

The first day back from the summer holiday, Mr. Verge—as his students called him—yelled at a couple of kids in the back row for talking and instantly reduced them to tears. Then he stalked menacingly over to the desk of another talker and turned both girl and desk around so that they faced away from the other students, effectively isolating her from her peers. Finally, since he didn't want to explain himself twice, he refused to let one little boy go to the washroom, with the result that the child had an embarrassing accident. It had been a pretty typical day.

That night, he went home to his solitary little bungalow. After supper, he settled down for his nightly brood. He liked to look back over his life and think about all the things that had gone wrong—it gave him a sharp, bitter pleasure to do this. But tonight was to be different.

Just as Mr. Verge had chosen to focus on a failed relationship from long ago (he relished the sense of self-pity it brought on), there was a sort of *poof* in a corner of the living room, followed by a rush of cold air. After the initial surprise that a *poof* could be chilling, Mr. Verge saw that there was a boy of about 10 years old perched cross-legged atop his stack of back issues of *Misanthrope Monthly*. Curiously, the child was dressed as a Victorian street urchin or Edwardian ragamuffin or something.

"Who are you?" snapped Mr. Verge.

"Name's Bud," said the boy, "and I'm a ghost—a ghost of Ira's past, you might say." He winked slyly and brushed his nose with his index finger in that absurd gesture that's supposed to mean, "You and me both—we're in the know."

"State your purpose," said Mr. Verge, with the same strict tone he used when saying, "Show me your homework."

"Simply put, to show you the error of your ways," said Bud.

"I'm not afraid of you," said Mr. Verge.

"I'm not afraid of you either," Bud said. "Now let's start with your yelling and general belligerence."

With that, Bud grew into a hulking giant at least 10 feet tall and dressed in a manner startlingly reminiscent of the local superintendant of schools, with whom Mr. Verge had often had words. Then, with a ghostly bellow that shattered Mr. Verge's brittle shell of false self-confidence, ghost boy Bud let him have it.

"WHAT IS WRONG WITH YOU, IRA? CLEARLY THERE'S SOMETHING WRONG WITH YOU, ONLY I CAN'T TELL WHAT IT IS BECAUSE IT COULD BE SO

MANY THINGS. YOU WON'T DO AS YOU'RE TOLD. YOU DON'T HAVE ANY FRIENDS. YOUR SO-CALLED LIFE HAS BEEN A COMPLETE WASTE!"

As well as the words, Mr. Verge could feel a blast of anger coming off the ghost—and it was actually painful. He felt awful, as though he had never been deserving of anything good and never would be. He felt unworthy—of what exactly he could not say.

Bud shrank back to his original size and appearance. "Now," he said, "let's see what childhood trauma could have led you to behave in this way. Oh wait—there wasn't any."

And there, playing out in front of him like a movie, Mr. Verge saw his parents, patiently negotiating with the stubborn, obstinate and ill-tempered child he had been. They never raised their voices or showed flashes of anger, but simply tried to work through things with him.

Now Mr. Verge saw that, having never been on the receiving end of a verbal scathing, he had no idea what being yelled at felt like. There was always a strictly professional atmosphere at the union meetings he had attended and always a generally polite atmosphere at the school. Although colleagues might have been critical, even urgent in their appeals to his better nature, he had simply never been yelled at the way he yelled at his students—and it did *not* feel good.

"And now," said Bud with the air of a midway barker, "let me introduce you to my friend in haunting, Solitary Sal." And with another chilling *poof* a sullen little waif-like girl was there beside Bud.

"What's going to happen now?" asked Mr. Verge. "What are you going to do to me?"

"Stop talking," said Solitary Sal.

"But I need to know what's going to happen next. I—"

"Stop talking," Sal said again.

"Please, I—"

But before he could get another word out, Mr. Verge felt himself violently swept up and spun around as though he were caught in a cyclone. Such was the force of the ghostly gale that his arms were flung helplessly about and battered him about the head and shoulders. It was terrifying—he had no control. Then he felt himself smash into a door, he was pulled back, the door mysteriously opened and he landed in a heap in his own closet.

It was a smallish closet, dark with no interior light. But he could tell it was his closet from the closety smell and because he could hear the unmistakable rubbery squeak of his stored galoshes rubbing together as he shifted his weight. The violence of the little whirlwind that transported him here had been startling and scary. Now another vision came to him, playing out in the cramped little closet as though he were in a theatre…

He was a child. It was Christmas or Thanksgiving or some other holiday and there was a family gathering and he was throwing some sort of tantrum up in his bedroom; he didn't want to put on his good clothes to come down and meet the company. In fact he didn't want to come down and meet the company at all. He remembered his parents discussing whether or not to hold him down and dress him, but they decided not to. They also decided that if he didn't want to come down he didn't have to—he could eat alone up here in his room. And so he did. Why had he done that? Why did he want to stay apart from everyone? Well whatever the reason, he had stayed apart from everyone, and that was what stuck with him.

Then, suddenly he was out in the living room again with the two young ghosts.

"How did you like being spun around violently and separated from everyone else?" asked Sal in an irritating little voice.

"Didn't like it at all," said Mr. Verge.

"Would you like some water?" asked Bud.

"Now that you mention it, I am very thirsty," Mr. Verge admitted.

Bud produced a pitcher of water and a large glass. He poured a cupful and Mr. Verge drank it down in one long pull. Being in the closet and seeing all of those visions had made him thirsty—having all these feelings had made him thirsty.

"More?" offered Bud. He poured another glass. Mr. Verge drank it. Bud poured another after that and Mr. Verge drank that one too.

Suddenly, Mr. Verge had to go and made for the bathroom.

"Where do you think you're going?" asked Bud.

"I'm just going to the—"

"No, you're not," said Bud.

Mr. Verge stopped in mid-step. Bud wasn't physically restraining him in any way, but nevertheless, he felt like he ought to obey. Still he had to go—really badly. But he knew that he wasn't allowed to. Bud wasn't allowing him to leave the room, and Bud was obviously a pretty powerful entity. It would be pretty embarrassing it he were to wet himself in front of these two ghosts, but at least he wasn't in the staff room at school with a bunch of other adults.

Suddenly though, Mr. Verge *was* in the staff room. He was standing in front of all the other teachers and they were regarding him suspiciously. He felt a warm, wet feeling crawling down his left pant leg.

"Ira, are you...all right?" It was the principal looking at him over her glasses with a mixture of pity and alarm.

"Should we call a doctor?" asked Miss Steinsky.

"Have you got a change of clothes here?" asked Mrs. Saunders.

Their calm, sensible concern made him feel more embarrassed than any mocking jibes could have done. Now he understood how the little boy had felt when Mr. Verge had not allowed him to go to the bathroom. Even worse, he couldn't actually remember the boy's name. Suddenly the teacher was back in his own living room, his pants still embarrassingly wet, Bud and Sal regarding him with raised eyebrows.

Then they were gone.

It wasn't exactly an overnight change—after all, a lifetime's worth of short-tempered bitterness doesn't exactly just disappear. But teachers and students alike noticed that Mr. Verge seemed to be...well...actually trying to consider the feelings of others. He started by apologizing to the little boy whom he'd refused to excuse to go to the washroom. And by the end of the school year, although everyone was still relieved to see him go, his colleagues and his students all noticed that he wasn't as quick to lose his temper and generally did so less often.

As for Mr. Verge, retirement beckoned, but it also loomed. He wasn't sure how he was going to fill his time. Initially, he'd looked forward to having more time to brood about how everything had gone all wrong, but since the visitation of the ghosts this no longer seemed like a such an enjoyable activity. Slowly but surely, the realization dawned on him that certainly there were times when things had gone wrong, but more often in his life it was he himself who had gone wrong. And, to his surprise, he felt that realizing this was something going right for a change. As retirement drew closer, Mr. Verge found himself spending more and more evenings not just wondering, but planning—planning how to make it go right.

The End